JAINA SANGA was [illegible] Mumbai. She is the author of a novel, *Silk Fish Opium*, and a collection of stories, *Train to Bombay*. Her stories and essays have appeared in *Asia Literary Review*, *Epiphany*, and *Southwest Review*, among other publications.

ALSO BY JAINA SANGA

Silk Fish Opium (2012)
Train to Bombay (2015)

'*Train to Bombay* is a walk down memory lane, a brilliant tribute to the city where Jaina Sanga grew up.'

—*Deccan Chronicle*

'*Silk Fish Opium* moves between the romantic and the political, a brisk leaping between genres. Extraordinarily gripping, the novel succeeds in reaching out to the emotional complexities of its characters and becomes a chronicle of Independence and Partition...An evocative, engaging novel...'

—*The Hindu*

'A beautifully written literary work of fiction...set in pre- and post-independence eras, the novel successfully creates the atmosphere of a young and aspiring India on the threshold of change and opportunities.'

—*The Asian Age*

Tourist Season

Two Novellas

Jaina Sanga

SPEAKING TIGER PUBLISHING PVT. LTD
4381/4, Ansari Road, Daryaganj
New Delhi 110002

ISBN: 978-93-863384-2-6
eISBN: 978-93-863384-1-9

10 9 8 7 6 5 4 3 2 1

Typeset in Adobe Garamond Pro by SÜRYA, New Delhi
Printed at Thomson Press India Ltd.

For my dear professors
David Anderson
and
William Siebenschuh
with admiration, respect, and gratitude

Contents

Tourist Season

It is always the same with mountains. Once you have lived with them for any length of time you belong to them. There is no escape.

—Ruskin Bond,
Rain in the Mountains: Notes from the Himalayas

The monkeys were back again. They screeched and pounded on the roof as if they were dancing in a wedding procession. Ramchander threw an irritated glance at the ceiling as he approached his desk and pushed aside some papers to make room for the three-tiered tiffin box. Just yesterday he had chased them away, yelling obscenities in Hindi and English, but there they were, back again, raising a ruckus. He rolled the chair closer to the desk, the casters squeaking and wobbling with age, and opened the tiffin box. Rice and egg curry. After nodding in satisfaction at the thick smell of garlic and green chillies, he frowned at the tiffin box's empty bottom tier. Suraj, his dimwitted manservant, had forgotten the carrot halwa again.

Ordinarily, he would have gone home for lunch, closing the shop for two or three hours and trudging up the hill behind the bazaar to his small cottage but today he had to tackle the accounts. Tomorrow was Saturday and the boarding school children would stream in to buy toothpaste and soap and bubble gum—he would be constantly interrupted. His gaze drifted to the shelves in the centre aisle, stacked with disorderly rows of jars of sweets and packages of salty snacks, and to the shelves along the wall crowded with boxes of disposable razors, cartons of milk powder, and bottles of this and that. He dreaded doing the monthly accounts.

He poured the egg curry over the rice and mixed it with

his fingers. After a few mouthfuls, he eyed the ledger on the shelf behind his desk, a fat blue clothbound book with RAMCHANDER PROVISION STORE written in his neat hand on the cover with a black felt-tip pen. The accounts would take the better part of the afternoon, but if everything tallied up he might be able to catch the five o'clock film at Picture Palace. He'd seen the film twice already and hadn't enjoyed it that much, but for a man of thirty-five, there was not much else to do in Mussoorie, this spit of a town at the foot of the Himalayas.

Halfway through his tiffin, he heard the front door rattle open. He looked up and saw a woman hesitating in the doorway. Although it was a cold day, the sun was out and he had wanted to prop the door ajar with a wedge, but those monkeys might descend from the roof and barge in. It had happened once before: two monkeys had walked in like kings, knocked over some shampoo bottles, and almost made away with a whole carton of Cadbury chocolates and a tin of Bournvita. Their intelligence and stealth—not to mention their vicious nature which contrasted sharply with their round pensive eyes—were not to be underestimated. The town supervisor had launched a campaign to relocate the monkeys to a faraway forest, and although Ramchander rarely agreed with the man and his policies, he had signed the petition. They would soon be rid of the pests.

Ramchander watched the woman contemplate the magazine stand near the door. A momentary breeze rustled the dated, lustreless covers and brought in a faint smell of burnt milk from the teashop nearby. She glanced with concern at the door—the glass was cracked and the frame discoloured—before letting it close. He could tell from the cut of her salwar kameez, the leather purse with its gold clasp, and the sunglasses pushed back on her head that she was not a native of the hill station. Here the people were less stylish. There were two cloth shops in the bazaar and four tailors—five, counting the tailor's nephew who sewed buttons. She was definitely a tourist.

The season didn't officially begin for another month, but Ramchander had noticed the tourist coaches from the plains were arriving earlier this year. On days when he went home at lunchtime he could hear, above Suraj's humming and the clanking of cutlery in the kitchen, the echo of buses roaring along the two-way road that spiralled up the mountain from Dehradun. He tried to imagine a pall of heat sweeping across the cities dotting the plains, the people perspiring like coolies, the parched earth turning brown and hard, but couldn't. He had spent all his life in this hill station and had never experienced the conspiracy of warm air and humidity that drove people from the plains to higher altitudes. Here it was winter that took people by the neck—the first biting air of December always felt as though the cold was alive and large and had a grip on them they would never be able to shake.

The woman shifted her purse from one arm to the other and stepped towards the shelves along the wall, her eyes scanning the paraphernalia. The way she held her head with her chin lifted, and the way she was standing now, with her shoulders back, Ramchander thought she must come from a wealthy family. She must have studied at some fancy college in Delhi or Mumbai, maybe even in the US, with a father who could afford the fees and pay for luxuries easily. Arching her neck, she glanced at the things on the top shelf.

Ramchander stopped eating, wiped his fingers on a rag he kept on a hook near the desk, and stood up. He was a good-looking man with a wide forehead, straight nose and deep-set brown eyes. But he'd let himself go, not caring about his appearance, often wearing the same clothes for days. He ran a quick hand over his dark hair and smoothed the front of his shirt. Enough daylight came in through the glass door and the windows at the back near his desk, but now that there was a customer he felt obliged to turn on the fluorescent tubelight, which started with a dim hum and added a weak glow to the space.

His shop was about twenty feet in length, a little less in width. There was no rhyme or reason to the shelves—boxes of Lipton tea stood next to bottles of Dabur hair oil. But he knew where everything was and when to restock. Whenever the boarding school kids asked for special items—calculator batteries, hair removing cream, deodorant spray, Horlicks or Bournvita, he would simply order them from his supplier in Dehradun and when the boxes arrived, he would unpack the contents on whatever shelf space was available. The floor, which he rarely swept, was still discernible as beige and blue mosaic, chipped in places, the grout lines grey with years. He ignored the cobwebs clouding the corners. He could hire someone to clean, but it seemed too much of a burden to organize. Once when a customer complained about the musty smell, he lit a stick of incense; the next day he unpacked cartons of washing soap on the shelves and after that couldn't locate the packet of incense.

The previous year, when Modern Provision Company set up shop at the east end of the bazaar, Ramchander was invited to the grand opening. There was a crowd outside, and he waited in line for almost an hour to enter. The new store was much larger than his, with polished wood shelves, colourful advertisements on the walls, and brands of shampoo and razors and cereals Ramchander had never seen before. There was a stack of plastic baskets near the door for shoppers, and two smiling cashiers standing behind two computers. A neon sign flashed along the back wall: YOU WANT IT, WE GOT IT. Ramchander was offered a paper plate and told to help himself to the samosas laid out on a festive tray. After eating two samosas, he wandered up and down the aisles, examining the products closely. An initial flare of jealousy was soon replaced with delight, and he took pride in the knowledge that the hill station was keeping up with the times. He watched the cashiers—two young men in blue, with the store's name embroidered on their shirt pockets—slide items over a scanner that seemed to register the item's price with a pert *ting*, and he noted their casual expertise at the computers. He briefly contemplated replacing the old Casio calculator that he used at his shop with a computer, but decided it would be too costly. After Modern opened, Ramchander's business dwindled; still, he made enough money to get by, and it did not occur to him to begrudge the new establishment or take measures to match the competition.

Each day after closing his shop, he could be found hanging out at the tea stalls, chatting with Hassan the tailor or Dilip who worked at Chik Chocolate or sometimes just a group of coolies. During the winter months he closed his shop at noon and spent his time tramping about the mountainside or brooding over a book at home.

Sometimes he whiled away the evening at Picture Palace,

the cinema house near the bus depot. Rialto was a better theatre, the seats were more comfortable, and he liked the classic English language films they showed. But once at Rialto when he had gone to see a Hitchcock film, the proprietor's daughter had followed him inside and sat next to him. A year older than him, she was a deaf-mute and had never married. Halfway through the movie, she had taken Ramchander's hand and put it on her breast, and then massaged his thigh, inching her fingers to the hardening bulge between his legs. After that evening, he avoided Rialto; people would talk, and he didn't see the point of starting something with her.

The tourist woman stepped this way and that, scanning the shelves slowly, without purpose or urgency. Whatever had she come to buy? She had glanced in Ramchander's direction when he turned on the light. He hoped she had not come for Stayfree or Femcare, which he kept in a cardboard box at the back. He had managed to overcome his shyness when the boarding school girls asked for these items—but a grown woman? 'Out of stock,' he would say now if she asked.

The tourist woman spotted something on the lowest shelf and he watched as she bent at the knees, keeping her back straight, her movements slow and poised. Her back was to him so he couldn't see what had caught her attention. Several moments passed before she turned to him, and asked, 'How much for this?'

Ramchander stared at the marble model of the Taj Mahal she was holding with both hands. How had she found that? His father had acquired the model when Ramchander was a boy; he didn't know from whom or where, but he remembered playing with it. It had been years since he'd seen it, and had forgotten it was there, half hidden by odds and ends and a big coil of rope. Just the day before, he had cut a yard-length of rope, but had paid no attention to the other things. He had knotted the rope on a stick to fashion a whip for the monkeys, and then marched upstairs to the narrow attic door opening onto the roof. There were almost a dozen monkeys, adults and youngsters with reddish-pink faces and rumps of the same colour. He thrashed the whip in the air, managed some sharp cracks, and shouted threats at them till his voice grew hoarse. The monkeys stopped, stared at him for several moments, and then, amazingly, grew quiet; a small band slunk away into the surrounding trees and the ones remaining scampered around on tip-toe, their heads drooping, their tails limp, the mischief gone from their eyes. Now Ramchander glanced at the ceiling. They were at it again—back to their usual rowdiness, whooping and jumping from the trees onto the roof in a mad game. The sloping tiled roof would collapse one of these days—some of the tiles were coming loose already.

The woman seemed oblivious to the commotion overhead. She turned the Taj around in her hands, keeping it flat, and inspected its sides. The monument sat on a square pedestal and the whole structure was etched with a filigree design. One of the four minarets appeared loose and she touched it lightly, trying to worry it back to symmetry. In the fluorescent light of the shop, the dome and the tips of the minarets appeared bluish-white. Holding it at eye level, she peered inside the model, and from where he stood, he got the impression that the filigree pattern was imprinted upon her face.

'Taj Mahal?' he said, stupidly.

'This is an unusual piece,' the woman said. 'Such intricate carving...but what's this, a light bulb inside the dome?' She held up the coil of thread-like wire trailing from beneath the dome.

He couldn't tell whether she was annoyed with the bulb or pleased. All he could do was stare at her fingers, which were thin and long, the fingernails shaped and painted carefully. He was reminded of his late mother, not because her fingers had been anything like this woman's—his mother's had been toughened and blunted with work—but because he knew this was the kind of woman his mother would have wished him to marry.

'It's genuine marble,' he said. 'The designs turn red and purple to match the changing angles of the sun, and the dome sparkles when the bulb is on.' He couldn't believe this forgotten toy had caught the tourist woman's fancy. Stepping closer, he saw the model was discoloured, and there was an irregular crack starting at the base and running halfway up the dome. 'I don't know if the bulb works.' He glanced toward the glass case at the back, which was empty save for some files he'd tossed in because he couldn't be bothered with the filing cabinet. If only he'd kept the Taj in the glass case. He could have used the glass case to display other things as well, for he felt sure there must be other such objects scattered around the shop.

'Where did you get this Taj?' she said. 'Is it for sale?'

'Sale?' He tried to recall a scene when his father had brought the Taj home and given it to him, but nothing came to mind. 'No,' he said. 'It's nothing really. It's just an old thing...this is a provision store, you see,' he gestured with both hands at the shelves. 'That Taj is just...well, what would you like to buy, Madam, talcum powder? Hair combs? I keep good quality items. Do you want sanitary napkins?' He turned his face in embarrassment. He couldn't believe he'd said that. 'Sorry, Madam,' he whispered to the wall. He never spoke to his customers like this—she must think he was a fool, or worse still, that he was trying to get fresh with her.

'No,' he heard her say. 'I don't need talcum powder or anything else.' He thought he detected irritation in her voice.

When he turned, he saw her squinting intently at the model. He watched her bend down, return it to the shelf. Her dupatta slipped off one shoulder, the gossamer fabric cascading to the crook of her elbow, and she pushed it back with her hand in a light, easy gesture. When she stood he saw the disappointment in her eyes, which were small and round and reminded him of the sweets he used to eat as a boy. Her shoulder-length hair was held back with two golden clips, and he liked the few streaks of lighter brown which he knew were created with special dye and which must be the latest style. Her face was clear and full, the cheeks dimpled around the mouth. His gaze drifted to her breasts and the tease of her hips. He looked away quickly, angry with himself for taking such liberties.

As she made for the door he caught a whiff of her floral perfume and for a moment he stood still, overcome with the feeling of new possibilities: he could trade his small life, living in the mundane simplicity of the hill station, for something meaningful and exciting and grand.

He looked down at his ill-fitting clothes, his brown

shoes with the broken laces he kept mending with knots, though he could easily have taken a new pair from the shelf and rethreaded them. He hadn't shaved in days. And those damn monkeys on the roof. His eyes scanned the shop, the chaos of the shelves turning his heart. Suddenly, he wished it were all in better order. He wanted her to see him in a different light. He wanted to spend his days with her, and his nights. He wanted to take her to the top of the mountain, sit beside her on the stoop outside St Paul's Church, and point to the town below: 'Look, there is the clock tower, the post office, the cinema, the bus depot.' He wanted to go with her to Meerut or Calcutta or wherever she was from. 'Madam,' he called out, as she was almost through the door. 'Please wait.' He rushed to the shelf and, picking up the Taj Mahal, said, 'You can have it if you want. I will see if the bulb works.'

~

Ramchander Provision Store stood near the clock tower, in the middle of the bazaar, just at the point where the narrow road dipped and curved before continuing towards the row of guesthouses and small eateries that came alive during the tourist season. The stoop in front of the shop was flanked with two mismatched flowerpots half-filled with dirt, dried leaves and cigarette butts. Built of brick and stone, the shop was attached to a Tibetan handicraft shop on one side, and stood next to an empty plot of land on the other. In the early 1800s, the plot had been selected as a laboratory site for Sir George Everest, the Surveyor General of India after whom the world's highest peak is named. But Sir Everest decided to set up his laboratory at Dehradun and, instead, built a large summerhouse in the hill station, not on the original plot but six kilometres out of town on a steep road barely accessible by mule carts. Some two centuries later, the land next to Ramchander's shop was still vacant. Monkeys frolicked in the sedges and swung from the branches of the old deodars that marked the perimeter of the plot.

The shop had belonged to his father, a serious, bespectacled man, who doted on Ramchander's mother, indulging her with trinkets and new saris whenever he had extra money. Ramchander had helped out at the shop when he was young, running errands for his father after school, or arranging tins of coffee and tea on the shelves. A thin, small-framed boy, he attended the hill station's government school and was the envy of his classmates: all those sweets and biscuits—could he really help himself to whatever he wanted? What he enjoyed most was when his father let him count the money at the end of the day: he would total up the coins and then watch in delight as his father licked his thumb and counted the notes so fast Ramchander couldn't even see his fingers. He liked to cut old pieces of paper to the shape of five- and ten-rupee notes, stack them in piles, and imitate the swish-swish of his father's fingers.

As Ramchander grew older, his interest in the shop waned. After he passed his matriculation exam, he wanted to leave the hill station. A whole world waited at the foot of the mountains. He was tall, his bony arms and legs had grown strong in the good hill station air, and the expression in his eyes exuded confidence. He contemplated applying for a job in the factories in Dehradun, or at the expansion site of the new Tehri Dam where they were training young graduates like him to become machine operators and foremen. Also, when he was a young boy he had been fascinated with electrical currents and voltages and how lines could short-circuit and now he contemplated going to college to study electrical engineering.

His father would hear none of it. The shop was *his* world; he thought it should be his son's as well. If Ramchander's mother were alive, she might have insisted that he attend the free government college in Meerut. With his fine penmanship and perfect score in mathematics, she would have wanted him to at least become a teacher at one of the boarding schools. But his mother had passed away suddenly of typhoid soon after Ramchander finished his matriculation.

So Ramchander was left with his father, and the shop. Most days, while his father tended to customers, Ramchander lounged at the back perusing magazines, listening to the cricket commentary and Hindi film songs on the radio, and ordering tea and snacks from the stalls nearby. His father, although prone to bouts of extreme and eccentric strictness, was not unkind, and Ramchander grew accustomed to his closed-mindedness. He realized one thing clearly: in his mother's absence, he and his father were inevitably and inescapably a unit.

When Ramchander was barely twenty, his father announced he was going to Delhi for a few days and leaving him in charge. Could Ramchander please turn off the radio, get his head out of the magazines, and pay attention to the customers? After a few cursory instructions, his father was gone.

A month went by, then two. Finally, Ramchander received a letter: his father had remarried and decided to stay on in Delhi. Ramchander could keep the shop or sell it and do what he wanted with the money. The news shocked Ramchander almost as much as his mother's death.

What had prompted his father's brash behaviour? Who was this woman that he had met and *married*? Was she someone his father had known earlier, and kept a secret from Ramchander—and his mother? As far as Ramchander knew, his father had always been faithful to his mother, and he had never been a man who did things impulsively. Moreover, his father had been wholeheartedly committed to the shop; not only was it their livelihood, but the shop was what defined them in the community. As Ramchander tried to make sense of his father's abandonment, he was shrouded with anger and sadness.

He stuffed his father's letter in the back pocket of his pants and, without locking the shop, wandered aimlessly through the bazaar, past the tea stalls and the mutton shop, past the bank and the barber. Eventually, he found himself on Camel's Back Road from where he climbed the steep steps to a rutted path and walked all the way to the top of the mountain. There he sat on the stoop outside St Paul's Church and, through eyes brimming with tears, stared at the town below: A hodgepodge of corrugated tin roofs pocked between tall pines and deodars, strips of road zigzagging through terraced tiered fields of barley and moong dal, and a rising reproachful mist that obfuscated everything.

The old Tibetan woman who owned the handicraft shop suggested he change the shop's signboard, which bore his father's name. Ramchander borrowed a ladder, took down the sign that read SURKUMAR PROVISION STORE and painted his own name over his father's, the old letters still showing through under the primer. Minutes after he put up the new signboard, Hoshyar, the town supervisor, roared up in a Jeep. He demanded ten thousand rupees to register the 'new' shop. Ramchander had no clue about business, the bribing and bargaining that went on, and paid the entire amount.

In those early years after inheriting the shop, Ramchander was overcome with the thick weighty sense of responsibility. He attended the town meetings in the large, high-ceilinged hall of the municipal building, sat in the front row and asked questions: What was the need to keep the tourist office open in the winter months? Why were they paying large sums of money to pump water from Dehradun when they could easily collect rainwater? Why were they allowing those long lines of trucks and bulldozers to plough down the trees on the ridge near the hill station? That last question drew gasps and more than a few chuckles from the assembly, as if he had asked a question even a child could answer. Surely he knew that the hill station needed more roads and houses. And there was even talk of a big luxury hotel.

For many years Ramchander opened his shop promptly at nine each morning, except on Sundays, and closed it in the evenings at eight, exactly as his father had done. He came to work in neatly pressed trousers and a white shirt, which was what his father always wore. In the monsoons, like his father, he rolled up his pants to his knees and waded through the muddy rivulets to the shop in rubber slippers, changed into the pair of socks and leather shoes he kept behind the counter when he got there, and donned the slippers again when he left in the evening. In winter, he brought out the small electric heater his father had purchased from an American missionary and, before plugging it in, remembered to tape pieces of cardboard around the cracks near the door where the frame had loosened from the brick.

Nobody in town talked about his father anymore, and if they mentioned him, it was only in a bad way, for having remarried so soon after his wife's death, and for having abandoned his son. Ramchander fervently hoped for his father's return. He imagined him entering the shop, surveying the scene with one hand on his hip and smiling proudly at the efficient manner in which his son was running the show. He often thought of going to Delhi to find his father and beg him to come home. But what would he say to his new mother? The months slipped into years and Ramchander didn't even make it down the mountain to Dehradun, let alone all the way to Delhi. The idea of simply selling the shop and leaving the hill station never entered his mind.

~

At the monthly town meeting, Hoshyar, a puffy-faced man, stood with his feet apart, reading from a clipboard, gesturing with his hands as he spoke. Of the forty-two people in attendance, the majority was in favour of his plan to relocate the monkeys. The man from the ministry of forestry, a thin fellow in a dark green uniform, standing beside him at the podium, was an expert on primates, but Hoshyar barely let him speak. Elections were approaching and Hoshyar wanted to become district supervisor. To win the citizens' votes he had already installed ten new lampposts along Library Road and commissioned repairs on the cable car that took tourists up to the observation point at Gun Hill. Now, if he dealt with this monkey problem, he was certain to be a hero.

The plan for moving the monkeys sounded good in its simplicity. Early in the morning they would set up cages at the end of the bazaar. The adult monkeys would be lured into the cages with food, while the smaller ones would be captured with nets. Timing was everything. It had to all happen simultaneously, before the adults could raise an alarm and send the youngsters skittering into the trees. The captured monkeys would be loaded onto trucks, driven to Uttarkashi, about ninety kilometres away, and released in the forest there. Hoshyar assured the crowd that the relocation project was easy and safe and completely humane. He turned to the man from the forestry ministry with a wide smile.

The man straightened his cap and stepped forward to speak. Keeping his eyes down, and speaking in a low tone, he said to the audience, 'Catching the monkeys is one thing, but loading, transporting, and freeing them is another matter.'

Hoshyar grunted and coughed, shook his head in disagreement.

The forestry official turned to Hoshyar and explained how opening the cages and untangling the nets would be tricky because, by then, the monkeys would be agitated and violent.

Hoshyar put an arm around the official's shoulder and said to the audience, 'It will be a little challenging. But believe me, if we don't do something, the problem will only get worse.' Hoshyar gave a graphic account of how a monkey had climbed through an upstairs window in his house, come down to the kitchen, and opened the refrigerator. 'Just think,' Hoshyar said. 'They know how to open the fridge!' Hoshyar's wife, who was frying puris at the stove, was so startled to see the monkey, she screamed, and toppled over the karahi with its hot oil. 'By God's grace,' Hoshyar said, looking at the priest and a few others in the audience who had a reputation for going to the temple every day, 'she narrowly escaped.'

Ramchander sat in what had become his usual seat in the back row, arms crossed over his chest, and listened distractedly to Hoshyar and the forestry official. He couldn't stop thinking about the tourist woman. Yesterday, while she had waited by the door, he had hurried to the panel of sockets and switches near his desk with the model of the Taj in his shaking hands. The marble pedestal was smooth to the touch and for a moment he imagined it was her palm resting in his. He pushed the tiffin box aside and set the model on his desk. With a pleading look at the dome, he straightened the wire, stretching it a little to reach the plug. Alas, when he flicked the switch, nothing happened. Inhaling sharply, he pushed the plug in more firmly, toggled the switch a few times and flexed the wire back and forth. But the bulb did not come on.

'I'm getting late,' the woman said. 'What's the price?'

Ramchander unplugged the wire and carrying the model in his hands as though it were a wounded bird, said, 'Madam, there is a small crack and it needs a new bulb.'

'There's no need for a bulb. It's a masterpiece.'

'Masterpiece?'

'Yes,' she said, irritation spreading on her face. 'The trouble…'

'No trouble,' he interjected. 'Madam, please, if you come back tomorrow or even later today I will see what I can do.' He looked at the floor, pressing his lips together, afraid she would decide that she didn't want this thing after all. If that happened, it would be the end of the matter and he would never see her again. When he glanced up, she nodded, and his breath caught in his chest.

'Tomorrow?' she said, tilting her head to one side. 'Shall I come back tomorrow? You will decide the price by then?'

He had no clear recollection of the next few moments. After she left, he paced the shop, every once in a while smoothing his hair with both hands or standing at his desk staring at the Taj. A few customers came in and he tended to them with a newfound eagerness. In the evening, after putting the 'Closed' sign on the door and bolting it from the inside, he set to work. Clearing his desk, he spread a sheet of brown paper over the wooden surface that was smudged with half circles left by glasses of tea. He ran both hands over the brown paper to smooth out the creases, and then placed the model in the centre. He found a desk lamp in the cupboard, angled the neck until the light fell just so, then arranged his tools evenly—screwdriver, penknife, razor blade, glue bottle, toothpicks, light bulb and wire. She had called it a 'masterpiece'. The word seemed large and elusive. *Masterpiece*, he kept breathing to himself as he chipped and chiselled and filed.

Now in the municipal hall, everyone was talking at once. Hoshyar was consulting with the official, who had told the assembly the forestry ministry was going on strike and there would be no staff available to carry out the work. Relocating the monkeys would have to wait a few weeks until the strike was resolved. Hoshyar shook his head angrily. 'Wait,' he shouted to the dispersing crowd, clapping his hands. He called for volunteers, 'some strong-bodied men to work the nets and ride in the trucks to Uttarkashi.'

The fruitwallah was the first to come forward. The monkeys around his shop were the worst. They would hide in the trees until he was busy with a customer, and then, just as he was accepting money and counting out the change, they would charge down in packs and knock things pell-mell from his shelves before making away with apples or baskets of grapes or a loom of bananas. Hoshyar thumped the fruitwallah's shoulder and tried to drum up more support. It was necessary for the well-being of the entire town, he said, and emphasized how it would take only a few hours to finish the job. 'Please, it is not so easy,' the forestry man kept saying. But Hoshyar ignored him.

Ramchander had long since given up taking any interest in the town's business. He only showed up at the meetings because they were compulsory and he didn't want to pay the fine, which he was certain Hoshyar pocketed. He was fed up with the monkeys, and he'd done his bit by signing his name to the petition. The priest from the Shiva temple had advocated leaving the monkeys alone. 'They are noble creatures, descendants of Hanuman,' he'd said. The old Tibetan woman had proffered the Buddhist belief that 'all life is sacred,' and while everyone was nodding complacently, added the premonition which had come to her in a dream: 'If you move the monkeys there will be mudslides and avalanches and all of Mussoorie will be wiped out.' Those influenced by the priest and the Tibetan woman had not signed the petition. But Ramchander was not a religious man; he went to the temple only on his birthday. And, he'd dismissed the warning about mudslides and avalanches as superstition.

Sitting now in the metal folding chair, he uncrossed his arms and leaned forward. Hoshyar was still at the front of the fast-emptying room. Ramchander wondered what the tourist woman would say about this project of monkey relocation. Certainly, it was a worthwhile mission. It might even be a danger-filled adventure. He rose from his chair and strode towards the front of the municipal hall. 'Hoshyar-ji,' he said, 'you can put my name down.' As Hoshyar looked at him with a mixture of shock and gratitude, Ramchander turned and walked away, a slight swagger to his step.

~

'Oh, my!' the tourist woman remarked upon entering the shop.

Overnight, Ramchander had transformed the place. He had dusted the shelves and swept the floor. Toothpaste and soap, hair oil and talcum powder, everything was arranged neatly on the shelves. Food items—coffee tins, soup cans, packets of sweets and biscuits—were organized on separate shelves from the sundries. The dented, torn, cardboard cartons were gone. Early that morning, he had rushed to Cambridge Bookstore to buy current issues of all the popular magazines, and replaced the old, dated ones he had with them. A new floor mat graced the entrance. In the brass cobra-shaped holder on his desk, a stick of sandalwood incense—he had found the packet behind a box of washing soap—stood at an artistic angle, waiting to be lit.

Ramchander shot up from the chair as she entered. In brown trousers, blue shirt and tie, and a woolen waistcoat, for it had turned cool again, with his face clean-shaven, hair trimmed and neatly parted, he cut a handsome figure. His hands shook a little as he struck a match and held it to the incense stick. Overhead, the monkeys were racing around on the roof, but he paid no attention to the noise. 'Please, Madam,' he said, gesturing with his hand, calling her to the back of the shop. 'It is ready.'

She stood by the door for several moments, her eyes taking in the newness. She was in a beige salwar kameez, a black shawl wrapped around her shoulders against the cold. From where he stood next to the glass case, he had the impression that she had materialized from a rare Mughal painting. She took her time walking towards his desk, glancing at the items on the shelves along the way. As she came closer he caught a whiff of her perfume, which he realized was different, perhaps just stronger, than the day before. He wanted to run his fingers over the fancy embroidery of her shawl. As he glanced at her sideways, he saw her looking at him with surprise. His heart raced faster and he wondered if he'd overdone it with the necktie. He touched the knot, tugged at his waistcoat. Turning away, he fished in his pocket for the keys and busied himself unlocking the glass case where the model sat on the middle shelf, as grand a replica there could ever be of the real monument that he now vowed to see someday. He should know the keys, but it took the third key to nudge the lock.

The more he tried to control his hands, the more they shook. Slowly he opened the case and brought out the Taj. It had taken some time to pry the dome off; since it was cracked he had had to be extra careful. He had replaced the bulb, mended the crack with fine brushstrokes of glue, and then polished the whole thing gently with the corner of a clean damp cloth.

He set the Taj on his desk, inserted the plug into a socket

and hurried over to the other wall to turn off the overhead light. Last night, after repairing the dome, he'd tested the new bulb a dozen times, but now a wave of doubt washed over him. What if he'd managed to blow up the bulb with all his testing?

In the muted darkness of the shop with the monkeys scuttling overhead and the sandalwood smoke lacing the air, he flicked on the switch. Pink and purple and blue, the colours danced on the dome, the minarets at the edges turned milky and iridescent against the glow. She gasped and edged closer to him, her elbow almost touching his. This unexpected intimacy shocked and delighted him. 'The price?' she said, then took a step back and looked straight into his face with unwavering eyes.

His face became a blank stare. It had not occurred to him to take money from her. Waving his hand in a dismissive gesture, he shook his head. 'Madam, it is a masterpiece, no?'

She nodded. 'I would like to buy it. Have you thought about the price?'

'Madam,' he said, 'I should like you to have it. Please accept it with my compliments.' He turned off the switch and as the colours faded, he walked to the other wall and turned on the overhead light.

She bent down and after inspecting the model, looked at him slowly. 'It is a very old model of the Taj,' she said in a quiet voice. 'Do you realize it is an antique?'

'Antique?'

'Yes. Seventeenth-century. This is probably one of the five original models built for Shah Jahan's approval by his marble cutters before the Taj was built. The other four are in a museum in Delhi. Well, actually three are in the museum right now, the fourth has been sent to Sotheby's in London for appraisal. I study antiques.' She lifted her chin a little and smiled. 'I run an auction house in Mumbai. We specialize in Mughal art.'

He kept staring at her, impressed by the confidence with which she spoke. 'I see,' he said, although he did not see at all. He could not understand how this Taj, discarded on an untidy shelf in his shop for years and only yesterday discovered by this tourist woman, could be an object of such historical significance.

'May I ask where you acquired this?' she said.

'My father…many years ago—I was a child then.'

'Did it always have a bulb inside?'

He scratched his head and looked away. 'When I was young, I opened the dome to fix the bulb inside…I liked to work with electrical things and knew some basic wiring. One day when I had nothing to do—' his voice trailed off. The memory of a long ago day came back to him in a punishing rush. It was the middle of the cold season, the days had surrendered their brilliance to a dismal fog and Ramchander, who was eleven years old, was waiting for his mother to return from hospital with his new baby brother or sister. He found a bulb, a socket, and some wire in the cupboard where his father saved odds and ends. After prying off the dome with a flat piece of metal, he positioned the socket and the bulb inside the model and glued the dome back on. His new sister—he was certain it was a sister because that's what he wanted—would like the pretty lights. But when his mother returned from hospital—carried on a stretcher, too weak to walk—she was silent; his father pulled him to his chest and kept talking, something about the baby being stillborn, that there would be no more children after this...Ramchander understood his words no more than he did the jabbering of the monkeys.

The tourist woman turned her attention to the model again. He kept staring at the back of her head as she brought her face to within a few inches of the dome. 'You really shouldn't have fiddled with this,' she said. 'I told you, there was no need to add a bulb inside. And, you shouldn't have repaired the crack.'

Ramchander's face crumpled. 'I was only trying to...' He sighed and stared at the floor. Overhead, the monkeys stomped and cackled.

She took a step back. 'Look, it's still a valuable piece.' She laughed lightly, and as Ramchander tried to smile, she said, 'You've repaired it beautifully, I can hardly see the crack. Of course, it would have been worth much more if...oh, never mind. What's done is done. How much?' She searched in her purse, pulled out her mobile phone and inspected it for a moment. 'You mustn't give it for free,' she said, slipping her phone back in her purse. 'In Mumbai, it would fetch at least...'

'Madam,' he said suddenly. 'I'm sorry about this noise.' He gestured with both hands at the ceiling. On the roof, two or three monkeys were having it out, he could hear them gnawing and snarling. 'Tomorrow I'm going with Hoshyar-ji, he's the town supervisor, and the fruitwallah and an expert from the forestry department. We're going to relocate the monkeys.'

'Oh,' she said, astonished.

He couldn't stop himself. 'We'll be setting up cages in the bazaar for the big monkeys and we have to pounce on the little ones with nets.'

'Pounce?' she said.

'Yes! And then we have to load them in trucks and drive to the forest outside Uttarkashi.'

'Oh,' she said again. 'Isn't it dangerous? There are so many monkeys here. How many will you catch?'

He shrugged and grinned, almost breathless with excitement. 'You are staying a few weeks?' he asked.

'Until Tuesday. I've come with a group.'

Tuesday. It was now Saturday. His heart plummeted, yet he smiled broadly. The monkey expedition was set for Sunday. At least he would have a chance to tell her of his adventures. 'Madam, what is your name?' he said, instantly regretting his boldness. What had come over him? What if she was married?

'Sonali. Here...' She searched in her purse again and produced a small silver box that opened like an envelope. 'Here's my business card.'

The card was beige with gold lettering, an address in Mumbai and below it her office and mobile numbers. 'Sonali,' he said theatrically, accepting her card. 'A Sanskrit name, it means "golden".'

She nodded.

'Did you ever think about taking a house here?' he said, 'A holiday home with a servant and all.'

She looked at him curiously. 'No,' she said. 'I've never thought about taking a holiday home here with a servant and all.'

The reiteration of his words stung him. 'Sorry...it was a silly idea.'

'Well, I might someday,' she said, and coughed a little.

'It has turned cold today,' he said. 'Would you like some

tea?' When she nodded, he pulled out his desk chair for her. 'A good hot cup of tea,' he said loudly to drown out the squeaks of the casters.

He hurried to the teashop next door. 'Don't skimp,' he said to the chaiwallah. 'Use the right amount of milk. And not those cracked glasses; I want cups and saucers, understood?' He told the chaiwalla's son, Sunder, a cheery-faced boy of ten or eleven, to bring the tea over when it was ready. 'Carry it nicely, don't spill it into the saucers.'

Raising his eyebrows, Sunder said, 'Why all this drama about the tea?'

Ramchander ignored him and kept walking.

'I know!' Sunder said. 'I saw her go into your shop. Is she a film star?'

Ramchander turned and looked at Sunder severely. 'No, of course not. She's in the antique business. She's come all the way from Mumbai to see me about antiques.'

'Antiques? What's that?'

Ramchander dismissed Sunder with an irritated wave of his hand.

When he returned to his shop, he found Sonali checking her mobile phone again. He stood in the doorway, disappointment flooding his mind. Was she committed to someone else? He straightened his shoulders and cleared his throat. 'Tea will be here soon,' he said, trying to sound jovial.

She continued with her mobile, punching the keys rapidly. 'Sorry,' she said after a moment and put the phone away. 'When I'm on holiday, I usually keep the phone off to save the battery.'

He glanced at the black telephone that sat on a shelf

behind his desk. He rarely used it. His father's phone diary, a wide-ruled exercise book with names and numbers written in pencil in no particular order, was still in the drawer below it. He wondered if he should invest in a mobile phone. All around him India was changing. He should keep up with the times. He imagined strolling through the bazaar chatting on his mobile, then turning it off with one hand and slipping it casually into his pocket. Most of the boarding school kids seemed to have mobiles. He would ask them which brand was best.

As though on cue, two teenage boys walked into the shop, both in school blazers. One of them asked for bouillon cubes and an immersion heater. Ramchander shook his head and suggested they try Modern Store, but they had already been there. He glanced at Sonali. This was not the time to ask the boys about mobile phones; she would think he was an ignorant fool. As the boys made for the door, Ramchander called out, 'My friends, I can order refreshments. Mango Frooti? Apple Fizz? What would you like?' Today he was the fulsome host. The boys hesitated, looked at him in surprise. 'Come, don't be shy,' Ramchander said. The boys shook their heads and said they must be on their way.

'The Taj?' Sonali said, gesturing to it with a little lift of her chin.

'Yes, yes,' he said. 'I will wrap it for you. I have a box ready.'

'But the money…'

'Don't worry about money. Here comes the tea now.'

Sitting upright in the chair with one leg crossed over the other, she sipped the tea delicately. 'Are you Ramchander?' she asked.

'Yes,' he said. He was standing next to her, wrapping the box in brown paper, his hands no longer shaking but folding and pressing the paper with measured assurance.

'The shop,' she said, and he looked down and met her gaze. 'The shop is much improved,' she said, holding his gaze for an instant.

He felt something ripple between them, an intimate moment, brief, but filled with opportunity. She had paid him a compliment and it set his heart pounding erratically. He knew he would never forget her words and the exact tone of her voice.

~

In the hazy pre-dawn light, Ramchander, clad in a thick sweater, a chequered scarf wrapped jauntily around his neck, hurried to the far end of the bazaar where he had agreed to meet the other men. The sun was rising grudgingly, sending mottled streaks of light across the dark Himalayan sky. The cold air clipped his ears and he wished he'd worn a cap. Thankfully, the northern wind coursing this stretch of the hillside, starting at the clock tower and sweeping along the narrow road, was sluggish this morning. As he walked past the shuttered shops and empty stalls it was hard to imagine the bustle of cycle-rickshaws, handcarts, and small trucks which would soon choke the road. Even the rooftops, he noticed glancing up, were peaceful, the monkeys still slumbering in the trees or on the mossy parapets of old houses. Ramchander slowed his steps and for several moments felt infused with a quiet sense of well-being.

The forestry man, whose name was Sampath, had set up ten cages in a large clearing past the dilapidated shed marking the end of the bazaar. The cages were positioned several yards apart, in a semi-circle. As Sampath checked the latches, Hoshyar followed him around, talking to his back. Both men waved as Ramchander approached. Hoshyar's sweater was stretched tight over his big belly. He'd brought a pith helmet, which he kept swinging about by the chinstrap. Sampath was in his forestry uniform—dark green pants, matching jacket with epaulettes and leather boots that came up to his shins. Two trucks and Hoshyar's Jeep were parked ahead on the narrow road hugging the mountainside, and the drivers of the vehicles sat on their haunches on the roadside, smoking beedis and rubbing their hands to keep warm.

'Where's the fruitwallah?' Hoshyar asked Ramchander.

'How should I know?' Ramchander said, adjusting the scarf around his neck, pulling it up to cover his ears, which were burning with cold.

He had never cared for the condescending, needling tone in which Hoshyar always spoke to him. Hoshyar might be fifteen or twenty years older, but that still didn't give him the right to talk in such a manner. He knew Hoshyar would boast at the next town meeting about how he had single-handedly dealt with the monkeys. Never mind, he would put up with Hoshyar today. He was excited for everything to begin. There would be much to tell Sonali. Sonali—it was a beautiful name. He must have smiled, because Hoshyar said, 'Ramu, you're in a good mood.' And that was the other thing Ramchander didn't like, the way Hoshyar called him 'Ramu', as though he was a house servant.

'Yes,' Ramchander said, dismissively. 'I'm in an excellent mood.'

Yesterday, just as Sonali was leaving the shop, the brown paper parcel in her hand, he asked, 'I was thinking…uh… have you eaten momos? Tomorrow we could go for momos in the evening, but only if…'

'Momos?' she said. 'What are momos?'

'A Tibetan delicacy,' he said. 'There's a stall in the bazaar, perhaps you've seen it already, the one with the orange flags and wooden benches in front?'

She looked at him in surprise for several moments. 'Okay,' she said, nodding her head and giggling.

After the monkey drive he would go home, take a bath, and put on his good clothes; he'd already laid them out on his bed. As they dined on momos, he would narrate the day's events.

From a nature book that featured a chapter on monkeys, he had learned they were hierarchical primates, obsessed with dominance of their territories and they spent a great deal of time establishing and maintaining rank. Females ruled the packs. If a female approved a supplicating male, he was allowed to stay and become part of the family; but if no female showed interest, his greater size meant nothing and the females would band together to chase him away. Ramchander planned to colour his account with this information when he met Sonali that evening. He had also read about the monkey's mating behaviour: females were known to mate with all the males in their troop. He chuckled, and decided to leave out such lewd details.

He wondered about inviting her to visit his house after dinner. He could ask casually, as though he had just thought about it that instant. His house, built by his father just before Ramchander was born, consisted of two small bedrooms and a living room with a sofa and two upholstered chairs, and a wooden dining table pushed against the window. The kitchen was at the back, beyond a short passageway, where some afternoons his man-servant Suraj spread a mat on the floor and napped. If Sonali accepted his invitation, he could show her the framed photo of his parents in their wedding regalia that still hung above the old sofa. But the more he dwelled on the thought of her visiting his house and, despite the bursts of hope and excitement that filled him, he concluded it wasn't such a good idea. She would think him too forward, and, more than that, his own nervousness got in the way. The anticipation of eating momos together and telling her about monkeys was thrilling enough for now.

'There's the fruitwallah,' Sampath said, pointing in the same direction from which Ramchander had come. 'Good, he's bringing bananas.'

The fruitwallah carried a large gunnysack on his back. 'Go, help him,' Hoshyar said to Ramchander. Ramchander shot him a sharp look. He had come prepared to take instructions from Sampath, he wasn't expecting Hoshyar to boss him around. But there was no point arguing so early in the morning so he trudged off to help.

The fruitwallah had brought two looms of bananas and some overripe apples. Sampath produced a large penknife from his pocket and cut the bananas off the first stalk. He left the other stalk half full and returned it to the gunnysack. He showed the others how to dangle the fruit from the cross bars at the back of the cages. Two cages were obscured behind a bush and Hoshyar was concerned the monkeys might not see them. 'Not to worry,' Sampath said. 'They're smart buggers.' The cage doors were designed to shut automatically. But it would be up to the men to rush and draw the latch, which was a complicated mechanism with a double-bolt to turn and a sliding bar to lock in place. Sampath would be responsible for four cages; Hoshyar, the fruitwallah, and Ramchander would deal with two each. Sampath had them practice the locking mechanism, then demonstrated the nets, which were as big as a bed sheet: 'Hold the corners like this, in a tight grip with your arms extended and then throw it over the monkeys, like this. If you do it right you can get five or six at a time.' The three men watched attentively and nodded. But as they practiced tossing their nets over imaginary targets, Sampath's face bore a doubtful expression.

'Okay, everyone ready?' Sampath said. He picked up the gunnysack with the half loom of bananas and strode towards the thicket of trees, about fifty metres away.

Ramchander, Hoshyar and the fruitwallah stood near their cages.

'Wait!' Hoshyar shouted.

Ramchander looked at Hoshyar, and saw him put on his helmet and tighten the strap about his chin. Ramchander turned away laughing. 'Hoshyar-ji, we're trapping monkeys,' he shouted over his shoulder, 'not shooting tigers.'

At the edge of the thicket, Sampath reached in his pocket for a small air pistol. He aimed it at the ground, and, as the shrill burst echoed in the cold quiet air, dozens of monkeys dropped from the trees. Sampath pulled out the half loom of bananas from the gunnysack, waved it at the monkeys and started running toward the cages.

The monkeys sprinted behind Sampath on all fours, their heads bobbing, most of their weight in their thin upper bodies, their arms doing most of the work while their short legs kept pace. In the early morning light their coats were surprisingly lush, almost golden, running patches of sun.

Ramchander was astounded by the large pack following Sampath—how were they ever going to capture them all? But there was no time to worry because suddenly monkeys were everywhere, jabbering excitedly, happily even. Ramchander, rooted to the ground, fear spiking his legs, saw the fruitwallah and Hoshyar spring into action. The next instant he heard the door of his first cage click, a moment later the second door. He swooped forward, turned the bolts and slid the bar through. To his amazement he had managed to catch a big male in the first cage, and a female clutching a youngster in the second. The male monkey, one ear chewed off, probably in some fight, started peeling the banana. The female, too, had got hold of the fruit, but seemed leery about eating it. The little monkey she held against her chest was asleep. Ramchander was struck by how different the monkeys were from each other, they each had their unique shape and colouring, their own expressions and bearing. He stood back, admiring his handiwork. It had been easy enough.

'The nets!' Sampath yelled. 'Get the nets.'

Monkeys were scampering everywhere, some climbing on top of the cages, some growling and gnashing their teeth. Ramchander managed to get two monkeys in the first net, two more in the second, and one in the third. Hoshyar and the fruitwallah had similar luck. Only Sampath had been able to trap five and six at a time. He had even tossed a net over three adult females who were feasting on the half loom he had left a little distance away.

Sampath waved and whistled to the truck drivers who were waiting to back the trucks into the clearing. Over much shouting of instructions—Hoshyar repeating Sampath's orders as though he was the expert—they loaded the captured monkeys. Ramchander climbed in beside Sampath in the front seat of the first truck, the fruitwallah rode in the second truck, Hoshyar in his Jeep, and the caravan set off for Uttarkashi.

'What's that for?' Ramchander said to Sampath, pointing to a large sheathed machete at their feet in the truck.

'In case of an emergency,' Sampath said calmly.

The sun was barely above the trees as they sped downhill. 'There are hundreds of monkeys still back there,' Ramchander said, pointing behind them to the hill station.

'It is a slow process,' Sampath said. 'It will take at least twenty more trips to make a difference.'

'Really?' Ramchander exclaimed. Why had he thought that this would be a quick, clean, one-time operation? Never mind. Right now he was feeling heroic and, despite his impatience with Hoshyar, he felt a sudden camaraderie with the men. Moreover, in a few hours he would see Sonali. He relaxed into the seat and chatted with Sampath about the social behaviour of *Rhesus macaques* as though he had been studying them for years.

Outside Uttarkashi, they stopped at a roadside stall for tea and bun-omelettes. Hoshyar complained that there were no onions in the omelettes. Everyone ignored him, but when Hoshyar kept on, Sampath said, 'Look around you. We're in the middle of nowhere. Do you see onions anywhere?' Ramchander was glad Sampath had spoken up.

Hoshyar wanted a second cup of tea, but Sampath said

they should get going; they had already spent far too much time at the tea stall and the monkeys would be agitated.

They drove on a gravel track towards the forested area. It started to rain and between the swish of windshield wipers, Ramchander spotted bursts of rhododendrons, pink and red and magenta like the dome of the Taj Mahal. He took a long breath: the smell of rain combined with diesel reminded him of the bus depot in Mussoorie. Perhaps he could convince the tourist woman to stay on a few more days. He could take her to Kempty Falls. She would enjoy the water leaping and somersaulting hundreds of feet down into the river. He would organize a picnic to Kempty... he must give detailed instructions to Suraj, remind him to prepare the carrot halwa. As the truck bumped along on the gravel road, Ramchander closed his eyes contentedly.

He heard the high-pitched yelps as soon as the trucks slowed. As Sampath directed the driver to edge the truck a few yards to the left, Ramchander scanned the smattering of birch and pine trees, scraggly bushes, and rocks. Where was the forest?

Sampath sighed and shook his head. 'I know. Deforestation is the main problem. Our division keeps planting new trees, but...' he opened the door and spat on the ground. 'Come on,' he said, jumping out. 'Our cargo is restless.'

The rain had turned to a misting drizzle, but the earlier downpour had left the ground slick and muddy underfoot. The monkeys' shrieks and cries made it difficult to hear Sampath's instructions. They started unloading the netted bundles, which looked like misshapen lumps of struggling limbs and heads, onto a large sheet of tarp.

When Ramchander grabbed the net, he could feel the fur of a monkey's back and the bony arm or leg of another. He shuddered and rearranged his grip, hoping he wouldn't get bitten. They dragged the tarp to a clearing and rolled the massive bundle off. They repeated this manoeuvre several times and then everyone stood back and watched as Sampath expertly undid the knots and the monkeys tumbled out. The monkeys kept shrieking and scampering around the men, who clapped and stamped their feet to shoo them off. Ramchander wished they had armed themselves with sticks to ward off the primates who were clearly not in a good mood after their ride.

Suddenly, Hoshyar was screaming.

When Ramchander turned, he saw Hoshyar crouched in the mud, the air full of fists and thuds. Two big monkeys were tearing at Hoshyar's sweater, scratching his face, and biting his arms. The cages were still on the trucks; these two must have managed to open the latches.

The next instant, Sampath was yelling and running towards Hoshyar. For a moment Ramchander stood useless, his hand on his mouth. Along with the truck drivers and the fruitwallah, he rushed towards Hoshyar. But Sampath gestured frantically for everyone to stay back.

'Go! Get it,' Sampath shouted at Ramchander, and pointed to the truck. 'Get the machete!'

Ramchander pictured the thing on the floor of the truck. He had nudged it a little with his shoe so he wouldn't have to rest his feet on it. *In case of an emergency*, Sampath had said. Was this an emergency? Ramchander ran to the truck, his legs wobbly, his heart thumping. Behind him, Sampath was yelling but Ramchander couldn't make out the words. *In case of an emergency*—the phrase pounded his head as he ran. He opened the truck door, breathless as he reached in and grabbed the machete. Surprised at its heft, he stood immobile, panting, wondering what to do next. Behind him the commotion raged on. He ripped the sheath off, gripped the black hilt with both hands, and, with the glinting curved blade pointing skyward, ran like a primitive warrior charging into battle.

Sampath had managed to kick one of the monkeys in the ribs, and it staggered back with a yelp of pain, glaring viciously at Sampath. It looked ready to lunge forward, but Sampath let out a bellowing growl, lifted his foot high in the air, and landed another hard kick. The monkey took a limping step, Sampath's boot had likely broken its ribs, and then it hobbled away, whimpering as it crouched on the ground a little distance away. The other monkey kept attacking Hoshyar, who was screaming and cowering, holding up his arms to shield his face. And there was Ramchander, suddenly two feet away, with the machete poised to strike. 'Do it!' Sampath shouted.

Ramchander's vision blurred. He saw a furry head and then the smooth brown surface of a helmet. What was he supposed to do? What was this thing he was holding? The handle was hot and coarse in his palms. *In case of an emergency*. A machete, he was holding a machete!

'Do it!' Sampath shouted again. 'In the neck. Now!'

Ramchander held his breath. The machete had a mind of its own. It came down heavily, crunching through bone and flesh. *Thoomp!* Ramchander would never forget the sound of the blade, the finality and power of it, the unfairness of it. He blinked at the ground, his arms twitched and slackened to his sides. Spent with the effort, he buckled to his knees and tossed the machete aside. Oh God, what had he done? Had he lopped off Hoshyar-ji's head?

He glanced at the fast-spreading pool of redness. Hoshyar was whimpering, sprawled in the mud, the stupid helmet crooked on his head. Beside him a monkey was writhing in agony, its tongue lolling out and its head flopping from side to side. A monkey with any fight left might have sat up and attempted even a haphazard punch as a last defence against imminent death, but this one lay slumped on the blood-soaked ground, its mangled head lifted slightly as though in a show of honour as it waited for the machete to come at it again and finish it off.

'Again,' Sampath shouted. 'Again, quick!'

Ramchander could hardly hear Sampath over the jabbering and screaming of the other monkeys who clearly sensed one of their own was in danger.

He managed to stand but when he tried a small step, he felt waves of blankness. Where was the machete? His balance thrown, he was about to keel over. He thought the dying monkey was looking him straight in the face, but the round eyes were dim and slow. The monkey made a tiny gesture, as though trying to raise a hand to touch its wounded neck. When Ramchander was a boy, a bully at school had wrestled him to the ground and gashed his forehead on a stone. Ramchander remembered how his mother had made a poultice for his wound with turmeric and water and a dash of salt. The monkey let out a low gurgling groan and Ramchander shut his eyes tightly. Several seconds passed, everyone around him was shouting but the monkey's groans were reduced to a whisper. Ramchander took up the machete and with his pulse beating in the hilt and the blade, struck the monkey again.

~

Sonali was already at the momo stall, sitting at one of the outdoor tables of the screened porch that was festooned with colourful lights. She waved at him and he realized with a start how much her loveliness contrasted with the events of the day. She was in a blue salwar kameez, and the black embroidered shawl from the day before. He noticed her dangling earrings, the bangles on her wrists. His heart rushed in delight. He slid onto the bench opposite her and, as the familiar scent of her eau de cologne came to him, he had the feeling she was his, and he had known her for years.

But as she chatted animatedly, he couldn't bring himself to match her mood. Around them, the daytime bustle of the bazaar was ending and in its place the hope of merriment beginning in the blare of film music and glow of lamplights sprouting around the hill station. From where he was sitting, he could see the evening sun dip into a filigree of leaves and a few minutes later, the sky grew orange and red and he could feel the touch of cold set in.

There were several other customers on the porch, a group of Tibetan teenagers, an older tourist-looking couple, and four young men who had already eaten and were drinking tea. No one Ramchander recognized. He had planned to introduce Sonali as a business associate from Mumbai should he run into someone he knew. They would gossip about him, of course, these small-minded people.

Sonali reached for her purse. He thought she was looking for her mobile phone, but she brought out an envelope and pushed it towards him. 'It's an expensive piece,' she said. 'I can't take it for free.' He didn't want to make a scene so he folded the envelope in half and slipped it in his shirt pocket, mumbling thanks.

He ordered their momos and when they were served, heaped onto two plates with sprigs of green onion and wilting cilantro, he watched her take a tentative bite. 'Ummmmm,' she said, her elegant fingers shiny with the grease of the momos.

'You like them?'

'Excellent,' she said, taking a bigger bite. 'I shall try using chopsticks.'

He looked on in amusement as she stabbed a momo with a chopstick. She giggled and, after another attempt, abandoned the chopsticks.

'Shall I ask for a fork?' he said.

She shook her head and started eating with her fingers. She told him she was reading a book about the Mughal empire. 'Shah Jahan was a visionary, a romantic emperor,' she said. 'How could his son be such a ruthless bastard?'

Ramchander wanted to point out that Shah Jahan had committed his fair share of atrocities; didn't she know the fate of the marble cutters once the Taj was completed? The emperor had had their hands hacked off. But who was he to judge? He was no better than the ruthless emperor. He had hacked off a monkey's head. Should he tell her this? He watched her dip a spoon in the bowl of sesame sauce and drizzle it over the momos.

'You're not eating,' she said.

He leaned forward and took a few bites, but he had no appetite. He looked around at the other customers and towards the small kitchen at the back. The gruesome event of the day, which in his mind did not even have a name, it was just that shapeless broken stretch of time that he found difficult to comprehend, kept feeding his sadness. He looked towards the small road, to the parked van impeding traffic, and to the sweet shop on the other side where the lights were blazing but there were no customers.

'Your expedition with the monkeys?' she said, leaning forward with interest. 'All went well?'

'Yes,' he said quietly.

'The monkeys are still everywhere. It doesn't look like…'

'It takes time,' he said.

After killing the monkey, he had collapsed on the ground, the machete still in his hands. A few moments later he heard Sampath shouting his name, and one of the drivers was shaking him by the shoulders.

'Buck up,' Sampath said to him, as he pried off the machete from his hands. 'Come on, we need your help.'

Ramchander watched the others load the bleeding, barely conscious Hoshyar into his Jeep. Sampath pressed a handkerchief to a cut on Hoshyar's ear but it kept bleeding. The driver said, 'Sahib's wrist is bleeding more than his ear.' Sampath pressed the handkerchief to Hoshyar's wrist and used a sock as a tourniquet. He instructed the driver to rush Hoshyar to Uttarkashi; they would follow in the trucks after unloading the remaining monkeys.

Ramchander staggered to his feet and did his best to help Sampath and the truck drivers unload the cages that were still on the trucks. The monkeys, their fists and feet clenched around the bars, were shaking and rattling the cages, and the stench emanating from them was unbearable. Ramchander wished he'd never agreed to this mission.

When they finished unloading the cages, he tapped Sampath's shoulder. 'Shouldn't we do something about—?' He pointed to the dead monkey. Several monkeys were circling and sniffing the area where the dead creature lay in a tragic mound. A small monkey was nudging it with both hands, as though trying to wake it from sleep.

Sampath pulled a shovel from the truck and tried to hand it to Ramchander.

'No!' Ramchander almost shouted. 'I'm not doing that.' He hurried to the truck and climbed in, glancing over his shoulder to see Sampath striding towards the dead monkey.

When they arrived at the hospital in Uttarkashi, Hoshyar had been taken into surgery. After an hour the doctor emerged and said Hoshyar had deep lacerations on his face, the muscles on his neck and shoulder were badly torn, and he had lost a lot of blood. Recovery would be slow.

'You saved his life,' Sampath said to Ramchander. 'If you hadn't run for the machete and killed the monkey, Hoshyar sahib would have been finished.'

Ramchander only stared at the floor, his breath labouring in jagged gasps. On the way back from Uttarkashi, he asked the driver to pull over. At the side of the road, he bent over and vomited. Overcome by nausea, he kept seeing images of furry limbs and tails.

When they returned to the hill station, news of his bravery spread quickly, and along the bazaar people stopped and waved at him. Even the Tibetan woman's old mother who couldn't walk and had to be lifted like a clay goddess, managed to crane her neck out the front door of her house and call out to him.

'I'm leaving day after,' Sonali said, dabbing a paper napkin to her lips.

He nodded slowly. 'The monkeys live in female-centered social groups,' he said.

'What?'

'The monkeys…' He sighed and shook his head. 'Never mind.' All those important details he'd carefully rehearsed lay clotted in his thoughts. 'Will you be coming back again?' he said, but even before she answered, he saw the slight movement of her shoulder, and read in the gesture the unlikely scenario of her return.

'You have my number,' she said. 'Phone if you come to Mumbai, okay? Who knows, one day you might find yourself opening a shop in Mumbai.' She laughed lightly, and he laughed, too, because he didn't know what else to say.

She insisted on paying the bill. He let her, too ill and demoralized to argue.

They left the momo stall and headed toward the main part of the bazaar, stopping briefly on the promontory from where they could see the big plain stretching below, everything coloured in moonlight, and Dehradun in the distance, a carpet of yellow and orange lights. While she exclaimed and gushed at the scene, Ramchander stood silent. All he could do was stare at the night, at the brightly dressed landscape that lay below and hope that this splendour might somehow bridge the world between them. When they resumed walking, he glanced behind him: The top of the mountain was capped in fog, the white stone steeple of St Paul's and the few houses around it completely invisible.

They walked to the end of the bazaar together and after they'd said goodbye, she took the road curving towards the row of guesthouses. He stood at the bend, watching her silhouette recede into the night.

At home, getting ready for bed, he hung his shirt on a hook on the wall and noticed the folded envelope in the pocket. She'd written his name on the front, and he stared at it for a few moments. The envelope wasn't sealed, she'd just tucked the flap under, and when he opened it and read the amount on the cheque, he was stunned. This much money for something he'd thought was a toy! Hurriedly, he stuffed the cheque back into the envelope. No, no, this was too much, he couldn't accept it. Sitting on the bed, he opened the envelope and looked at the cheque again. It was drawn on HSBC Bank and there was no mistaking the amount.

He got into bed, but couldn't sleep. He lay on his back under the blankets, his palms under his head. He didn't know for sure how much money it would take to open a shop in Mumbai, but the figure on the cheque seemed like a lot—he had never imagined that he, Ramchander, would ever hold a cheque for that kind of money in his life. There might even be some left over to buy a second-hand car. He didn't know how to drive, but he would learn. He imagined driving to Sonali's house in a car, picking her up, and taking her to a movie. He imagined them sitting in a café being served by uniformed waiters. She would have brought a file folder that she would set on the table, angle it towards him, and together they would study images of sculptures and figurines. He believed he had a good knowledge of Mughal history—he had read both volumes of *The History of India*—and would proffer his advice on Mughal antiques. His confidence grew large and brash and soon he was all aquiver at the thought of putting his hands on her waist and feeling her body against his.

~

The next day he walked to the top of the mountain: a solitary figure, his head bent in concentration, hands clasped loosely behind his back, moving slowly through the pines and deodars, the heels of his shoes leaving hexagonal imprints in the soft mud.

At the top of the mountain he sat for a while on the stoop outside St Paul's Church. The morning was brisk and bright and he could see all the way down the valley. He listened for voices talking or singing inside the church, he listened for the grunting of a mule, the echo of a truck's horn, but there was only the susurration of the wind through the trees. He stretched his legs into the sun and flexed his ankles.

Some thousand feet below, on the steep zigzagging road, traffic moved at a slow pace. He tried to pick out a tourist coach travelling downhill. He imagined her at a window seat, her big sunglasses on her face, and the wind blowing her hair. He recalled her voice, her face, and the little breath she took when she smiled. He recalled the great novelty of her presence in his shop. But it was no use. The silence and the brilliance of the morning were bigger and more profound than his paltry memories.

Sometimes he felt the mountain was a living creature, something big and brave with mind and muscle; it could be gentle or malevolent depending on its mood. On a bright warm day when the mountain stood with resplendent stillness, there was an easy symmetry between his thoughts and the colour of the sky and the smell of the air. But when the trucks and buses rumbled along the road, he could feel the mountain breathe. When the bulldozers on the far ridge pulled and ploughed, he could sense the mountain shaking its giant head. Opening a shop in Mumbai sounded exotic, and, more than that, to be with Sonali, to claim her as his, was what he desperately wanted; but all said and done, the mountain was bound up with his life and he could not bear the thought of leaving it.

From inside the church came the sound of someone opening a window. A man leaned out and said 'Hello! Good morning! Want to come inside?' Ramchander couldn't see who it was, but he waved and said he would be going now.

On the way back to the bazaar he took the long way, around the north face of the mountain. In the distance, hundreds of kilometres away, he could make out the snow-capped peak of Bunderpunch, Monkey's Tail. Indeed, the entire ridge curved like a tail. He walked slowly—he wasn't tired, but he needed to catch up with himself and put things properly in place. The path sloped steeply downhill and he could feel the steady pressure in his knees.

Rounding a bend, he came upon two monkeys. They were sitting on a flat boulder to one side of the path, barely ten metres away. The larger monkey was stroking the smaller one, picking fleas from its back, and examining its ears. Ramchander stared in amazement…such slow, unhurried gestures, yet every movement of the grooming ritual seemed infused with an ancient efficiency. Ramchander kept very quiet, certain that if he so much as exhaled, they would screech and scamper off. It came to him then, the realization that it was wrong to move the monkeys from the hill station. They ran riot on his roof, foraged the town's rubbish, and stole from the fruitwallah. But, sending them to a denuded forest where they would surely die…wasn't it too harsh a response to a minor annoyance?

Ramchander took a small step forward. He had to get past the monkeys, but startling them might make them angry. He coughed to make his approach known, and stamped the ground more deliberately as he took another step. Both the monkeys turned. He expected them to leap off the boulder and make for the trees. But they sat still and quiet, eyeing him. He edged closer. A couple more steps and he could slip past and be on his way down the path. The monkeys started chattering, the smaller monkey held out a hand, palm upward, and beckoned to Ramchander, as though he was a friend they were waiting for. Ramchander raised his eyebrows and shrugged his shoulders in reply. The monkey inched closer and to Ramchander's surprise, imitated the gesture. The larger monkey started jabbering loudly, hopping from one foot to another and moving both arms in big synchronized swoops. For a moment, Ramchander had the urge to do the same. He turned hurriedly and started walking downhill, not so fast that it would seem as though he was fleeing, and when he was a safe distance away, he threw a glance over his shoulder and saw that both monkeys had left their perch and were bounding away in the opposite direction.

When Ramchander returned to the shop, he sat at his desk. He had brought his tiffin, but it was too early to eat lunch. The ledger was still on his desk. He hadn't even begun the monthly accounts. He opened the drawer below the phone and brought out Sonali's business card that he had placed on top of the exercise book that had been his father's phone diary. '*Sonali*,' he said aloud as he studied her address and phone numbers and ran his fingers over the raised lettering. One of these days, when he bought a mobile phone for himself, he would order business cards just like hers, gold lettering on a beige background. He picked up the receiver and as he dialled her number, he held an image of her standing in his shop, peering at the Taj Mahal—a seventeenth-century antique! Made for an emperor! Pressing the phone to his ear, he cleared his throat and waited. He heard the ring tone twice, then a beep and the line went silent. He smiled…she must have turned it off to save the battery. He returned her card to the drawer, centering it within the blank area of the exercise book's cover meant for a label, and closed the drawer softly.

The River

The Ganges, above all is the river of India, which has held India's heart captive and drawn uncounted millions to her banks since the dawn of history. The story of the Ganges, from her source to the sea, from old times to new, is the story of India's civilization and culture, of the rise and fall of empires, of great and proud cities, of man's adventures...

—Jawaharlal Nehru,
Discovery of India, 1946

1

Terror seized him, a sharp icy bolt. 'Careful, the steps are steep!' someone behind shouted, but his heel had already missed the edge and his leg was turning outward. He was slim and lithe, but even as he lifted his arms for balance like a high-wire acrobat, the bowl in his hands with offerings of marigolds, sugar, and rice flew through the air. He was falling...falling...down the steps...face forward, eyes focused absently on the moving water... panic spreading through his body. The bowl landed with a dull clang amid throngs of pilgrims, beggars, and vendors.

He must have fainted because when he opened his eyes, he found himself splayed on the ghats of the Ganges, his torso tilted downward, his arms outstretched. He felt as though he had been falling all his life. The river flowed on, rapid and reckless, cluttered with the detritus of some upstream storm. A blazing sensation seared his forehead, and he gasped and blinked at the rude gush of blood, his blood, spilling onto the stone steps and into the silt-heavy river.

At least he had stopped falling, at least he was on firm ground, and hadn't been washed away in the current. It was a glorious feeling, not to be falling anymore. The world was a kind place, and he felt at ease in it.The sun was coming up over the river, bringing a hazy saffron glow to the temples and shrines. A mild breeze carried the smell of ancient mountains. He took a slow breath, marvelling at how air filled his lungs. Nearby, a bald shirtless man sitting on his haunches at the edge of the water was gargling and running a finger over his teeth like a toothbrush. Two women were bathing in the river, one immersing her body fully, her wet sari clinging to her voluptuousness; the other, tentative, self-conscious, cupping her hands and splashing water on her face.

When he tried to raise himself to a sitting position, he found his hand dangling in the river. He spread his fingers to the gentle catch and pull of the water…he could let his fingers play here for a while. Dipping his hand in further, he felt the water becoming fast and thick. Countless years ago the Ganges, too, had fallen—she had come tumbling out, violent and impetuous, from Shiva's matted hair.

Someone was pulling him up and propping him on the steps as though he were a puppet stuffed with sawdust. He felt strong hands grip him by the armpits. He looked down at himself and saw his white shirt mottled with dirt and blood. That earlier bout of terror returned and brought with it a headache, a pounding like a pickaxe chipping and chiselling at his skull. 'Girnar! Are you okay? Answer me!' said a voice he was sure he recognized, though could not place. A cloth was pressed to his forehead to staunch the bleeding. His legs felt loose and disconnected from himself. People were crowding around him. 'Bring ice.' 'Move aside.' 'Hospital!' The words swirled in the space above his head. He closed his eyes. To die in Benares, was this not every Hindu's dream?

~

Girnar Chabria was from Ahmedabad, a dusty maze of a city that had grown as a textile capital during the bygone days of the British Raj. The black soil found in abundance in the surrounding area was perfect for growing cotton and there was enough water and cheap labour to power the mills.

While his father and grandfather had worked in textiles, Girnar read religion and philosophy. After his graduate exams in which he scored 'Distinction' in all six papers, he took a job teaching mythology at the Government College of Gujarat. He struggled his way through the ranks from junior lecturer to senior, and it was only after a research stint when his treatise 'Integral Consciousness', tracing the connections between Hinduism and Existentialism was published in a foreign journal, that his colleagues stopped calling him 'Mister Chabria' and he became 'Professor-ji.' But he was never sure of their tone: was it respect or sarcasm that laced the way they addressed him?

He lived in the Paradise Plaza Housing Complex, a squat seven-storey structure looming over a warren of rundown buildings and shops near the National Highway. Weathered blue paint covered the outside, the balconies barely wide enough to hold a flowerpot were strung with clotheslines, and television antennas and satellite disks crowded the rooftop. Inside, a tiled entrance hall funelled into a passageway leading to a lift with a sliding cage door. Girnar usually avoided the lift, which smelled of perspiration and the liftman's hair oil, and opted for the narrow staircase beyond meant for the servants. His flat was on the second floor, so the stairs were only a minor exertion. Filled with a hodgepodge of furniture purchased from kabadiwallahs, his flat was a mess of books and papers.

His aging parents lived in the flat opposite his, across a dingy hallway where a wooden statue of Ganesh sat on a pedestal in the corner at the turn in the stairs. Girnar went over every morning and evening, for breakfast and dinner, which his mother prepared with the help of a part-time servant boy. His parents went for walks every day, ate heartily, and took no medicines other than a sticky, sweet-smelling homeopathic tincture touted to promote 'good body & temper'. His mother, a round-faced cheerful woman in a bright cotton sari and a large red bindi on her forehead, worried about her son's unmarried status and blamed herself for not finding an appropriate girl for him.

Some thirty years ago, when Girnar was eighteen, he had fallen secretly in love with his cousin, Nalima. She was his father's brother's daughter, a year younger than him. His uncle lived in Delhi, so he only saw Nalima during summer holidays and sometimes during Diwali. They played badminton and went to the cinema, and one night in Delhi when they were alone on the terrace of his uncle's bungalow, she let him hold her hand. They sent each other birthday cards and occasionally spoke on the phone. Alas, one day, Nalima met a Muslim boy at her college. She went to a mosque, changed her name to Nafiza, and married the Muslim. When Girnar learned what Nalima had done, he was stunned—not because the fellow was Muslim, but because he had assumed some day, even though they were cousins, he and Nalima would be married. A few weeks after her wedding, he heard Nalima-Nafiza had moved to Pakistan. Girnar never saw her again.

Each time Girnar's mother had tried to arrange a marriage, inviting one charming girl after another, accompanied by her parents, to tea at the Gymkhana Club, Girnar could only think of Nalima. Now he was forty-eight and, though by general Indian standards past the marriageable age, his mother constantly brought up the topic and prayed she might still find a suitable girl for him.

Girnar's father worried about his son's job, which was in jeopardy because of the dwindling number of students who took his course. 'Mark my words,' his father said, 'India's future is in heavy machinery and petro-chemicals. My son, you made a big mistake. You should have gone into engineering or chemistry. Mythology is a useless subject.'

Girnar was not the sort to panic; he knew the mythology department would ultimately close, but until then, he might as well make the most of it. So he appeared in the lecture hall, every day except Sunday, in ironed shirt and pants and single-knotted tie, stood before his ten or twelve students, and spoke extemporaneously on Vedic texts, his voice echoing in the large room as a few heads nodded off. After class, he ate his lunch in the college canteen—the rice and dal plate, or a packet of tomato-chutney sandwiches—and spent the afternoon in the library at a dilapidated colonial mahogany desk at the back, past a long row of carrels. There was a big tamarind tree outside the window and sometimes he stared at the knobby elongated fruit and listened to the sparrows rustling about in its branches. If he let his mind wander, he was certain to start thinking of his cousin Nalima. With a tightness growing in his throat, he would wish he had claimed her from the beginning, been a little more direct, a little more daring.

One day he was walking about the library to clear his mind when he came upon a vast section marked 'Novels in English.' Compared to the 'Mythology' section—three short, dusty rows, no more than nine linear feet altogether—there were hundreds of books on these shelves. He went past this section every day to get to his usual desk, but had not really paid much attention to these colourful spines. He picked a couple of books at random and perused the pages quickly. As a teenager, he had read some novels in school, but couldn't recall the titles, let alone what they were about. What he remembered about his English class was Mrs Saldana in her too-tight skirt-blouse and high-heeled sandals, and the other boys whipping out their fountain pens and shaking them in the air behind her back as she went down the rows of desks, winking and giggling as the ink streaked her buttocks. He carried an armful of novels to his desk, pushed aside the fat mythology journals and started reading.

With the approaching summer vacation, he took a stack of novels home and studied them closely, inserting used envelopes or bus tickets or chits from the corner shop to mark exceptional prose. He was struck by the certainty and confidence of some writers, as though what they were writing was something they'd thought about and dreamt of for many years. He read and reread passages that caused a jump of delight in his chest, or wrenched his heart with a profound and expansive sorrow. He tossed aside writers addicted to bombastic language, or those who relied too much on cause and effect. He was titillated at first by descriptions of intimacy, but could soon differentiate between what was genuine and organic and what was gratuitous. Love, he had always thought, was a rare and profound emotion and he had no use for writers who made careless reference to it. He skipped long descriptions of hot weather, but lingered over cold places. When he had finished reading, he sat at his desk with sheets of paper and copied out excerpts from his favourite novels. As he filled up each sheet, he taped it to the wall. Soon all the walls of his flat were covered with exemplary passages. He wandered around the flat, reading these excerpts aloud, trying to absorb their tone and style and rhythm.

By the time the air in Ahmedabad turned cooler and the kite-flying season drove everyone to the rooftops, Girnar had started writing a novel. Rising before dawn and working in rumpled white pajamas at a small table in his messy flat, drinking cup after cup of tea, he was overcome with a newfound sense of purpose. Often he was late for his morning lectures at college, appearing in a dishevelled state, face unshaven and hair uncombed. He let the afternoon classes out early, and hurried home to work on his novel. He patterned the story of his hero and heroine on his own unrequited love affair with Nalima. Creating a novel was difficult. Instead of deconstructing the fantastical Hindu myths to which he had devoted his career, he was forced to think more realistically, more reasonably. Once underway, he was determined to finish. It wasn't because he thought he had uncovered some grand truth about the world or arrived at some deep understanding about life and death, but because he couldn't stand the suspense of the story he was creating. He was startled by the way the characters took over, and he was dying to know whether the heroine, forsaking her husband in Pakistan would return to the hero in India, or whether, by novel's end, the hero would discover that loving her had been a mistake from page one.

~

Girnar had been curious when he read the notice in the entrance hall near the lift: *Ganges Pilgrimage. Information meeting. Sunday: 10 a.m. Tea & biscuits provided.* He knew immediately that it was Niranjan who had posted the notice for he was always organizing picnics and excursions to concerts and plays for the building's residents. Girnar's parents often went on these outings, but Girnar, who was somewhat of an introvert, always made some excuse. He read the notice again. Should he attend the meeting? He had never seen the Ganges before, and this might be a good opportunity. He knew about the holy cities in north India—he was a professor of Hindu mythology, after all—but wasn't it high time he visited these fabled places?

Niranjan, a grey-haired, retired stockbroker and solicitor, lived on the top floor of Paradise Plaza, from where the view of the mostly low-rise city threw into stark contrast the relative affluence of the building's residents compared to the poverty amid which they lived. On days when the wind blew away the haze of smog one could see the squalid squatter camps along the National Highway, home to the poor people that clung to the city for a livelihood and were regarded as successes in their distant impoverished villages, even as they worked the public rubbish bins for discarded bottles, cans and anything that might be worth a rupee or two.

Niranjan was president of Paradise Plaza's building association. Every month he hosted a meeting at his flat. The same three or four residents showed up each time, but Niranjan, dressed in white silk kurta over beige pants, stood by formalities and called the meeting to order. He worked through the month's agenda—the cracks in the compound wall, the electricity meters that sparked and fizzled when it rained, the sloping area at the side of the building meant for a water-garden, which even after a decade of discussion had not materialized—and afterwards wrote up the minutes of the meeting, which he hand-delivered to all the building's residents, inviting himself in for a cup of tea or a cold drink.

His wife had passed away some years ago, and his daughter, Samira, lived with him and looked after the flat and her father as best she could. Rouge-faced and perfumed, hair slipping from its clip and falling around her neck, her fair skin and pretty features might have launched her in the movies, but in her mid-twenties when she had gone to Bombay to audition, wearing a sequined sari, halter-style blouse, and red stilettos, the Bollywood director said the Indian audience preferred full-bodied heroines and she was a little on the thin side. She put away the stilettos and went into medicine, and was now a pathologist at Civil Lines Hospital. She was popular with the building residents who routinely sought her advice for ailments ranging from common colds and upset stomachs to lung, kidney and heart conditions. They stopped her in the passageway near the lift, or at the compound gate, and even as she reminded them that she was a pathologist and they should seek the advice of a cardiologist or a gastroenterologist, they embarked on their medical history and pleaded for her opinion.

That Sunday, the chatter that filled Niranjan's sitting room gave the place a festive atmosphere. Samira had underestimated how many would respond to her father's invitation—a small pot of tea was sufficient for his usual meetings—and now she was a flurry of activity in the kitchen, yelling at the servant to run down to the corner shop for more biscuits while she prepared more tea and hunted for cups and saucers. In the sitting room, Niranjan stood with his feet apart, coiling the edge of his moustache, and smiling broadly. 'At least once in our lives,' he said, raising his index finger, 'we must bathe in the Ganges and atone for our sins!'

He had planned a fourteen-day pilgrimage to the headwaters of the Ganges with stops at five holy cites: Benares, Allahabad, Haridwar, Rishikesh, and Gangotri. The trip to Gaumukh Glacier was optional; it involved a long, difficult trek from Gangotri.

Everyone wanted to go. Those who had been on pilgrimage before boasted with opinions and questions: fourteen days were not enough, fifteen would be ideal; the pilgrimage ought to start in Patna, not Benares; the traditional route included Kedarnath and Badrinath, why was Niranjan taking everyone to the source of the Ganges? And, why go to north India when the temples in the south were so much more beautiful? Niranjan maintained a calm authority. Some said he was charging too much, what was the need for a chartered bus? And, why stay in hotels when there were plenty of ashrams and small resthouses along the route? It was a pilgrimage after all, not a luxury tour.

After the initial meeting many dropped out—small children and those deemed too old were discouraged because the trip would be arduous. The final list was whittled down to twelve: Niranjan, his daughter Samira, their servant, Jadu, four other couples, and Girnar Chabria.

~

At the ghats, two passersby lifted the bloodied Girnar and carried him to the road. Niranjan helped him into a cycle-rickshaw and told the driver to rush them to the nearest hospital.

The rickshawallah, eager to rise to the occasion, and perhaps earn some extra baksheesh, trilled the bell on his handlebars, yelling to the pedestrians and stray dogs to get out of the way. As they gained speed, he flashed a grin and broke into song, '*Mere sapnon ki rani kab aayegi tu...*' It was from *Araadhana*, a classic Hindi film. Girnar slumped down, images of the film's stars, Rajesh Khanna and Sharmila Tagore, dancing behind his eyes. Niranjan pressed the white handkerchief, now dark with blood, more firmly onto his forehead and shouted at the rickshawallah, 'How far is this hospital? Go faster!' The fellow pumped his legs harder for a few seconds and as the cycle-rickshaw rattled on, he gave the bell a few more merry rings and resumed singing.

They stopped in front of a dilapidated building wedged between a small welding shop and a fruit stall. 'Hospital,' the rickshawallah announced, pointing to a sign that read *Benares Medical Clinic*. Niranjan beckoned two men sitting on the footpath and with their help, managed to get Girnar inside. Striding through the waiting room filled with people slumped in chairs or reclining on the floor, Niranjan approached a uniformed assistant at a desk who directed them into a small examination room where a bed was draped with a blue vinyl sheet.

A man in a white coat who everyone called Dr Aziz and who spoke a combination of Hindi and English, pronounced that no X-rays were necessary as Girnar was talking normally and knew his name, the date, and where he was. 'It's only a mild concussion,' Dr Aziz said.When he left the room for a few moments, the nurse disclosed that the X-ray machine was out of order, but assured them that Dr Aziz was the best doctor in Benares. Dr Aziz returned and wanted to know exactly where and how he had fallen. Girnar lifted his hand and gestured weakly at Niranjan to provide the details. Dr Aziz examined his limbs, his neck, his spine, pressed his stomach, measured his blood pressure and pulse. Turning to the nurse he said, 'It's remarkable that the patient doesn't have any other cuts or broken bones.'

Dr Aziz asked the nurse to ready a syringe of Lidocaine, and she hunted in the drawers, and then left the room. She was gone for almost ten minutes and Dr Aziz grew tired of waiting. 'It may hurt a little,' he said, tapping Girnar's arm, 'but you're a strong fellow.' The gash on Girnar's head took seven stitches to close. He squirmed and ground his teeth each time he felt the needle, and once in a while Niranjan squeezed his arm and murmured something in sympathy. The sutures were dabbed with iodine and Mercurochrome and his head was wrapped with a big gauze bandage. Dr Aziz handed him a sheaf of pills. 'Take two, or three, for pain. No more than six a day. You can buy more at a medical store when these run out.'

Outside the clinic, as they waited for another rickshaw, Niranjan patted his shoulder. 'So lucky you are,' he said. 'Did you see the current? You could have fallen in and drowned. Goddess Ganga was looking out for you.'

Girnar touched the bandage with both hands, moved his fingers hesitantly around his head. Had he been that close to the water? He glanced at Niranjan and was surprised by the martinet expression on the older man's face. Niranjan nodded, then looked away. Girnar stared at the side of

Niranjan's puffy neck, at the few stray hairs growing from his ear. He could have *drowned* in the Ganges? The mythical kings Sagara and Bhagiratha had performed great austerities to bring the Ganges down to earth. He wanted to say something profound, but all he could think about was his mouth, his lungs, and his brain filling with the river and his body sinking into its murky depths.

~

The Benares Guesthouse was a two-storey building that sat on a narrow lane behind Assi Ghat, the southern-most ghat in Benares, where the Ganges makes a wide sweeping curve to the north. They had arrived here only yesterday: twelve pilgrims with twenty-nine pieces of luggage—suitcases, duffle bags, bedding rolls, plastic buckets and cardboard boxes packed with homemade snacks.

Girnar went directly to his room. His head hurt.The bandage felt tight. The room was sparsely furnished, a table by the bed and two mismatched chairs. His suitcase was propped on the bigger chair. The nametag on the suitcase, which he had made from an old greeting card, was now smudged and tattered. On the wall opposite the bed was a sink with a good mirror, and next to it, curiously, sat an old-fashioned sewing machine. He placed his sandals on the flat foot-control of the machine. Opposite his room, down a short corridor, was a bathroom with an Indian-style toilet. He sat on the bed and pushed his fist into the sagging mattress. At least the sheets were white and he could see from the creases that they'd been laundered and ironed. He propped the thin pillow against the headboard and lay on the bed with one knee drawn up, the sheet covering him.

As he began to doze off, he was pulled back by a knock

on the door and his companions crowded into his room. In Ahmedabad, he kept his distance from them, only nodding or offering a cursory greeting whenever he encountered someone near the lift, or at the bus stop. News of the building residents came to him via his mother who attended the Ladies' Monday Tea held at a different person's flat every fortnight and at which news was exchanged of illnesses, marriages, births, deaths, jobs started, jobs lost, the twists and turns of TV serials, the rising cost of sugar, oil, milk, even bananas, and all the other mundane goings-on of small lives. Girnar's mother reported and deconstructed the news over dinner that same evening. The more sensational news, which always seemed to involve Niranjan or Samira—for instance, Niranjan getting stabbed with a knife one night in the luckless alleys of Ahmedabad by a band of thugs allegedly hired by a politician who was angry because Niranjan might contest his parliament post. Or, Samira's two broken engagements, the first to a rising film actor who turned out to be a playboy, the second to a businessman who was indicted for bogus land deals in Dubai. The stories kept his mother enthralled for several evenings.

Now here was Samira, sitting at the edge of Girnar's bed. She was small-framed and doll-like, an unlikely physique for a pathologist, who Girnar thought should be full-figured and robust. She was his age, more or less: mid forties. Once Girnar's mother had suggested Samira as a suitable match—such a *sweet* girl, and since she lived in their building, the whole arrangement would be so *convenient*. But his mother never invited Samira and her father for tea: Girnar had turned down all the other girls and if he refused Samira, it would put the two families in an awkward position, not to mention all the babble in the building that her son's refusal would generate.

Girnar shifted his legs to make space at the end of the bed, but no one else wanted to sit so he stretched his legs again. At first everyone spoke in hushed voices. Samira kept eyeing Girnar with concern. Perhaps he needed a blood transfusion, she said to her father, who shrugged and shook his head. Girnar sighed and turned his head to the wall; he had become a burden to them. Their attention made him self-conscious, and he didn't like the way they were talking about him in the third person, as though he were a child or in another room. Samira discussed intracranial bleeding, haemorrhage, the risk of a stroke, and this alarmed Girnar, but Niranjan waved his hands in dismissal and said with a laugh, 'Just look at him. Except for that bandage, he's a picture of health.'

Soon the room filled with loud chatter. Girnar, head pounding despite the three pills he had taken, smiled dully at his fellow pilgrims as they offered advice and regaled him with tales of their own injuries. Niranjan lifted the hood of the old sewing machine and declared it to be in excellent condition, speculating that the usual occupant of the room must be a tailor forced to temporarily vacate to make room for the pilgrims. He dropped the hood down with a thud, causing Girnar's head to hurt even more. Niranjan suggested he try to sleep; Jadu, the servant, would be posted outside his door, should he need anything. The pilgrims spilled out into the compound and Girnar could hear them talking and laughing through the open window above his bed.

What a fine way to begin a journey. He kicked off the bedsheet, letting half of it trail on the floor. Tucking his hands under his neck, he stared at the ceiling. His eyes followed a thick black wire that led to a light fixture. He could see dead insects inside. Did he really care about going to the source of the Ganges? From what sins was he seeking atonement? He couldn't think of any. What came to mind instead was his first novel, which he had got professionally typed on first quality bank paper, then packed the manuscript in an old red sari box and sent it via registered post to a publisher in Delhi. He wanted to write another novel, a contemporary story invoking ancient Hindu myths. He wanted to make a name for himself as a mythological novelist. It was not money he was after—he didn't even know how much his books might fetch. Of course, if it was a sizeable sum, he could buy a bungalow in a verdant hill station like Simla or Darjeeling, hire a servant, a cook, and a gardener, and spend his days roaming around looking at the trees and listening to birdsong. More than money, it was prestige he coveted. He was tired of being a professor of a useless subject. He wanted everyone in the college staff room to look at him with respect. He wanted to stand at the podium of a lecture hall full of students who would clamour for his mentorship and whisper in awe as he strolled the halls. He wanted *recognition.*

His first novel was too literary, too quiet, he concluded; it lacked intrigue and pathos. But his second novel, which would move through great sweeps of Indian history and present a whirlwind of disasters and triumphs with a generous sprinkling of eroticism and romance, was certain to become a hit. If the publisher asked for a sequel, he would refuse at first and expound on dream memory and artistic inspiration and whatnot. He would walk and talk like a writer and cultivate the persona of an eccentric man. He had work to do in Ahmedabad. He recalled reading the advice of a prize-winning novelist: *To write a good book you must sit at your desk and work till your back is sore and your bum hurts.* Instead, here he was, laid out on a narrow bed in a dingy room in Benares with a bandage on his head.

When his parents heard of his accident they would be frantic. Usually he had little patience for their endless discussions about what his goals and ambitions ought to be and the casual way they pointed out this or that person's achievements—but right now he longed for their ministrations. He was their only progeny, named after a mountain peak on the Gujarat peninsula where his parents had gone on their honeymoon. Girnar, his namesake, was 950 metres high, with dozens of temples solemnly lining the way to the top. When he was young, he often wished his name was Girish or Gopal—even George for that matter—anything to prevent his schoolmates from calling him 'parvath,' the Gujarati word for mountain. He didn't know why it bothered him—it wasn't such an insulting word, after all—but it did.

Turning on his side, he pulled the sheet tightly under his chin and closed his eyes. Tomorrow he would take the night train back to Ahmedabad. Everyone would be disappointed, especially Niranjan. 'We *need* you on the pilgrimage,' Niranjan had said the day he had gone to the meeting in his flat. 'You're a scholar of Hinduism, you will be an asset…' Niranjan had put his name at the top of the list. Now Girnar imagined the pilgrimage route and the sights along the way—Vishnu's footprint at Haridwar, thousands of oil lamps afloat in the river at sunset, the swinging bridge at Rishikesh, the glacier at Gangotri—and downplayed everything in his mind. He reached for the glass on the bedside table, held it to his lips, but returned it without drinking. Water from the Ganges was holy but it also harboured a rich brew of pollutants: he could come down with dysentery, typhoid, or cholera. He could *die* from just a sip of Ganges water after narrowly escaping drowning in it.

~

Sitting around a rickety table in the centre of the guesthouse's courtyard, the pilgrims gathered for dinner. A wide doorway festooned with wilting yellow flowers and mango leaves led to the kitchen and a curved wall marked the perimeter of the compound. A large neem grew near the wall, its roots and trunk in the courtyard, its branches hanging over the lane outside.

Girnar found himself next to Samira. Glancing at her blue salwar kameez, he was glad he had changed into a clean shirt for dinner. Although he wasn't a large man—he was thin but muscular, his shoulders well proportioned to his chest and lower body—he felt big and awkward next to Samira, and his bandaged head didn't help matters. Despite her small frame, he noticed in the way she sat upright in the chair that she was not timid, and that she had a healthy appetite, eagerly taking large servings of each dish laid out on the makeshift banquet table, which had been covered with an embroidered tablecloth.

Niranjan spoke about the onward journey. Some of the others complained about their sub-standard rooms, and the lack of attached baths. Niranjan appeased their complaints by reminding them it was the pilgrimage season and, except for five-star hotels, everything else was booked solid. Did they want to pay five-star prices? Girnar listened half-heartedly to the good-natured banter, waiting for an appropriate moment to announce his intention of returning to Ahmedabad. He looked around the table at the odd cast of characters. Each of them, he was sure, had some strange proclivities.

The idea came to him in a confident surge: if he stayed on the pilgrimage, he could write about these people. Based on what he saw and heard along the way, he could turn his fellow pilgrims into fictional characters. It had been done before, writers borrowing characters and storylines from here and there, and adding a bit of this, a bit of that. The opportunity was staring at him and he would be foolish to ignore it. His mythological novel and its many sequels would have to wait. Right now he must focus on a book of stories, pounding headache notwithstanding. He surveyed the table again, more slowly this time. These pilgrims could be transformed into folk heroes, in their stories he could render a microcosm of modern India's journey towards self-realization.

Girnar sat up straighter, forgot his throbbing head, and helped himself to two more puris. He would carry on and write another book. He would be the best pilgrim in the history of all pilgrims. He longed to announce his project to the others, but decided it might cause unnecessary problems; conscious of his role as an observer, their behaviour would change and they might start dictating what he should and shouldn't write.

Samira tapped his elbow. 'Professor-ji,' she said, 'You're eating well. You must be feeling better.' Girnar only half-heard her words; his suddenly clear mind was occupied with stories and how best to structure his book. A new project should begin by invoking the elephant-headed Ganesh, the God of Wisdom, Patron of Letters and Mover of Obstacles. Tomorrow he must remember to look for a Ganesh temple and put at least a hundred rupees in the donation box.

'Yes,' he said, pressing his foot firmly on the cobbled ground, and added in an undertone to her: 'I'm going to write stories.'

'Stories?'

'Stories about the pilgrims, about everyone here.' He couldn't help himself. 'I'm going to write a book,' he said in a low voice.

'A book,' Samira narrowed her eyes. She spoke quietly too, sensing the need for a degree of confidentiality in his strange but thrilling declaration. 'You have brought your computer?'

'No, I don't have a computer. I'm going to buy one next year. I'm waiting for the new model to come out.'

'So, then how—'

'Pen and paper!' he said. 'I'll send Jadu to the shops tomorrow to buy some notebooks.'

'Have you ever written a story before?'

'No,' he lied. It had been seven months and thirteen days since he had sent his novel to the publisher. He pictured the manuscript buried under a random pile on an editor's desk in Delhi. He resolved to send a letter of inquiry as soon as the pilgrimage was over. It had taken a long time to write that novel, and admittedly, there were some parts he had rushed through, where the writing was somewhat sloppy. The editor might be forced to reject it, flat out, but he didn't care. He had struck upon a new idea and was confident and eager to get started. India stretched before him, a vast complex tableau waiting to be distilled into words.

'Want my help?' she said. 'I do like to read, I could make suggestions…'

'No!' He drew back from the table. 'That won't be necessary. But, thank you all the same.'

'You don't look like a writer,' she said.

'I don't *look* like a writer?' Should he grow a beard, or wear thin-rimmed spectacles and a frayed woollen coat? Should he sit in a chai shop every evening, smoking cigarettes and pondering the world? He met Samira's eyes cautiously.

'Well, maybe you do,' she said with a shrug, then turned to talk with someone else.

He took another puri, carefully selecting a puffy one from the platter. He imagined his book—three hundred pages, printed on good paper, a colourful cover—lining the shelves at Crossword Books and that bookshop in Alpha Mall he had yet to visit. He would donate a signed copy to the college library. Taking a deep breath, certain he was on the right path, he marvelled at how smoothly everything was falling into place.

~

That night he couldn't sleep. He could hear Niranjan snoring in the next room. How could a person snore so loudly? He heard a low bellowing outside, a cow or a buffalo, and then in the distance, the erratic clamour of bells. What temple was open at this time? Didn't the gods deserve their sleep?

He fumbled for his watch, which he had slid under the pillow. He aligned it on his wrist, hooked the strap into the buckle and snapped the clasp. It read five minutes before two o'clock. He raised a hand to his forehead. The bandage. When he was young, a firecracker had misfired and, just as he turned to run, the thing had exploded, searing a small streak along his leg, just below the knee. He remembered the way his skin tore open, and how the flesh, purple and grey…oh, but now he was going to write another book! He got out of bed, tightened the drawstring of his pajamas, slipped a shirt over his singlet, and found his sandals.

Through the courtyard, down the short path that led to the main gate, and then he was out onto the deserted lane, the smooth warm night in his ears. Although he couldn't see a moon, the sky was clear and bright, with stars or the city's own electrical brilliance, he couldn't say. He walked aimlessly. A dog huddled outside a shuttered shop looked up, barked once, and put its head down again. At a food stall, chairs were upturned and roped to the tables. The lane was going toward the river, and getting narrower to a point where two people would find it hard to walk side by side. A few metres on he saw a signboard illuminated by a fluorescent tube.

Tulsi Ghat, the sign read in English and Hindi. A short flight of stone steps went down to a house. It was a typical dwelling, small, run-down, like the others in its row. It seemed abandoned. On the wall to one side of the front door were two barred windows with foggy discoloured glass. He pushed the door even though it had a rusty padlock on it. The door heaved and creaked, and from inside came a faint scuttling—rats, probably.

Could it be that four centuries ago the sage Tulsidasa had written the *Ramayana* here? He imagined a gaunt old man, a huge tilak on his forehead and strands of holy beads around his neck. Creeping to one of the windows, he peered inside. The place was empty. He imagined Tulsidasa sitting upright on the floor, his papers in disciplined stacks, and his face intent. He stepped back from the window, amazed that such a monumental work might have been written in such an ordinary house. But he was letting his imagination run, just because this was Tulsi Ghat didn't mean this was Tulsidasa's house. He was about to leave when he heard the sound of footsteps coming down the lane. Slinking into the building's shadow, he held his breath.

A woman in a salwar kameez appeared on the steps.

Did she live here? 'Hey,' he called out.

She gasped loudly and stood rooted on the second step, scanning the darkness.

He edged forward, assessing her in the shadowy light cast by the fluorescent tube on the sign. She was a foreigner, he realized.'What are you doing here?' he said, more boldly than he intended.

'I'm sorry,' she said. She turned, took a step backwards, tense and ready to flee.

'Do you live in this house?' he said.

'No,' she said, her voice shook a little. 'I was just walking. I couldn't sleep. I'll go...'

'Wait,' he said, moving out of the shadows. He stood about five feet from her, his hands on his hips. 'Do you know whose house this is?'

'I don't understand your question...I didn't mean to bother you...' she said, fear palpable in her voice.

'It's okay,' he said, 'Do you live nearby?'

'No. I'm sorry to intrude,' she stammered. 'Please let me go now.'

He came closer. Her hair was shoulder-length and her dupatta was tied athletically at her waist instead of draped over her shoulder. He imagined she was in her forties, but he wasn't sure. He heard the sharp intake of her breath as he took another step towards her. 'Relax,' he said, holding both his hands up, 'I'm not going to harm you!'

'Your head,' she said, pointing to the bandage.

'It's nothing,' he said, touching his forehead. The pain had devolved into a low, gnashing ache. 'I fell on the ghats this morning.'

'I'm sorry,' she said. 'I fell, too, yesterday. I bruised my elbow.' She lifted the injured arm.

'Then we have something in common. You're American?'

She hesitated, then turned and started up the stairs hurriedly, glancing over her shoulder to see if he might be following her.

'It's not my house,' he said, gesturing behind him with his hand. 'I'm staying at a guesthouse nearby. I've come with a group from Ahmedabad. We're on a pilgrimage. I also couldn't sleep.'

'Oh.' She relaxed a little on hearing he was a pilgrim and stopped on the steps.

'Where are you from?' he said. 'Is this your first time in India?'

'I was born in India, in Lucknow. My family left when I was seven. I've come back to…'

'Ah, to connect with your birthplace.'

'Well, yes, I suppose. I'm here for work. I really must go now.'

'Work? What work?'

'I'm a writer…'

'Really? A writer?'

'Yes, a writer.'

How easily and definitively she pronounced the word. He cleared his throat and bowed slightly. 'May I ask your name?'

'Katherine.' She half extended her hand. 'Mrs Katherine Morrison,' she said in a formal tone.

'You write novels?'

'Heavens no,' she said with a laugh. 'I write historical pieces, travel essays, human interest reports, that sort of thing.'

'Then you could write about this.' He pointed at the house, and even though he had no idea if it was true, he said authoritatively, 'This is Tulsidasa's house. He wrote an epic. Do you know the *Ramayana*?'

'Yes, I've heard of it.' She took a long breath, then sat on the step and bent towards her feet. He noticed her white canvas shoes. It struck him as odd for a woman in a salwar kameez to wear such shoes.

'The *Ramayana* has 24,000 rhyming couplets,' he said. 'It conveys the *essence* of Hindu culture and philosophy.'

She nodded and started retying her shoelaces.

He tried to speak more casually. 'In the sixth century, the saint Valmiki composed the original epic in Sanskrit. Only the priests could read it. Tulsidasa translated it into Hindi and brought the story to the common people.'

'I see.' She leaned forward and putting both palms on her knees, prepared to stand. 'I'm here to write about the river. I work for a magazine.'

'Are you from New York? Chicago? Los Angeles?'

'I'm American, but I live in London...'

'And you were born in India. You are an *international* person, Mrs Morrison.'

She laughed. It was an easy, confident laugh. 'I never thought of myself that way,' she said. The next instant she shot to her feet, as though that earlier fear at having encountered a stranger in the middle of the night had reared up in her again. 'I must be on my way now.' She climbed the rest of the steps, and once she got to the top, she turned and seeing that Girnar had not followed her and was a safe distance away, raised her hand to wave.

Girnar waved back and stood for a few moments watching her silhouette recede into the night.

With his bandaged head bent in thought, his steps slow and deliberate, he made his way back to the guesthouse. He prided himself for having seen Tulsidasa's house—by now he had convinced himself this was indeed a fact. Was it a sign, coming upon it so randomly? The gods were validating his decision, showering their blessings upon him. And, he had run into this intriguing foreign woman, a writer, no less. He smiled, put his hands in his pockets and glanced at the sky. Indeed, his book would be grand.

Back at the guesthouse he lay in bed, drifting in and out of sleep. How would he structure the book? What about the title? Maybe he could write thousands of pages and make it an epic.

2

Girnar trudged with the group for two kilometres along the river, stopping at temples along the way, wishing he had pen and paper to begin his work. He would have to wait until Jadu had time to fetch the supplies. Every time they approached the ghats, whoever was at the front, turned and shouted: 'Professor-ji, please be careful.' He acknowledged the concern with a wave and made a show of putting both feet on each step.

It was the first week of September, the monsoons just over, and the river hummed along, full of vigour. Ash-smeared sadhus meditated on the steps, despite the jostling throngs trying to get to the water's edge. Girnar watched a man in white shorts wade in, bend his knees slightly, close his eyes and pinch his nose, and then disappear underwater. He stayed submerged for a long time, and Girnar got a bit worried. When he emerged, he raised both arms to the sky and shouted, '*Ganga maiya ki jai!*' He repeated this manoeuvre several times. There was a grace and flow to his movements. Girnar could have stood there all day watching him.

A band of small boys, their naked bodies glistening with water, dived in to retrieve pilgrims' offerings of coconuts, ornaments, and gold and silver coins. The coconuts would be wiped clean and sold to the next pilgrim, the coins and ornaments pocketed. Today there was no policeman brandishing a stick and warning the boys about the dangerous river current.

Benares was the city of Shiva, destroyer of the ego and the universe, the personification of the third branch of the Hindu trinity. Niranjan led them to temples he claimed were the most important. Some were crammed with people, some virtually empty. Inside, Niranjan enlisted the head priest who droned on about the ubiquitous Shiva lingum, the phallus-shaped stone anointed with flowers and incense and symbolizing creation. Every now and then Niranjan asked if Girnar had anything to add, any bit of mythological information to deepen the experience, but Girnar shook his head, anxious to move on.

On the way back Girnar walked beside Samira through a crowded bazaar. As they approached a boy sitting at the side of the road selling trinkets, the boy waved his arms and held up a necklace made of carved wooden beads. 'One hundred rupees, not a paisa less,' he said with a grin. Samira offered him twenty rupees. 'Okay, twenty,' he said unabashedly. He took the proffered notes and was about to wrap the necklace in newspaper, but instead, thrust it at Girnar and, with a wink, urged him to put it on Samira. Girnar stared at the necklace in his hands, unsure of what to do. He looked severely at the boy, but the boy only grinned and winked again. Girnar held the thing tentatively, as though it was made of precious jewels instead of the cheap trinket that it was. Samira smiled as she turned her back and lifted her hair out of the way and before he knew it, there he was, standing on the footpath fastening the necklace on her. As his fingers brushed the back of her neck, he drew a quick breath at the small current that raced up his arms.

The group had gone ahead and he wanted to catch up, but Samira insisted on stopping at a silk emporium.

'I'll wait outside,' he said, trying not to look at her necklace.

Sitting on the stoop, he contemplated buying a sari for his mother. Benares was known for its silks. But he had never bought a sari before. He peeked inside the shop. To his amazement, there, perched on a stool, was Mrs Morrison. A notepad on her lap, she was talking intently to the owner, a grey-haired, well-dressed man with gold-rimmed spectacles.

'Mrs Morrison!' he called from outside and entered the shop smiling, his hands extended in greeting.

The silk emporium was a long stuffy room with neatly folded saris piled to the ceiling. Mrs Morrison was interviewing local business owners about the river for her magazine. She was dressed again in a salwar kameez, the dupatta tied at her waist like a belt, and her canvas shoes. A cloth bag crammed with books and a camera sat on the counter, next to a half-empty glass of tea. The owner snapped his fingers at someone at the back, called for another glass of tea for Girnar, and then excused himself for a few minutes to answer a phone call.

Girnar chatted easily with Mrs Morrison. They had met only the previous night, but talked as though they were old family friends.

Samira was preoccupied with the saris, and he called her name loudly, keen to introduce her to Mrs Morrison.

'Mrs Morrison is a writer for an international magazine,' he said to Samira, pronouncing 'writer' with emphasis, hoping some of the grandeur might reflect on him.

They shook hands and exchanged pleasantries while the shop assistant kept unfurling saris, pointing out the patterns and the embroidery, eager to reclaim Samira's attention. After her interview with the shopkeeper, Mrs Morrison said she was headed to the area around Malaviya Bridge, to see the old city of Kashi. 'Would you like to come?' she said suddenly, looking first at Girnar and then at Samira.

Girnar let out a small gasp, he felt important at the spontaneity of this invitation from a foreign woman. But he must make it clear he was not attached to Samira, who was only another pilgrim in his group.

'No,' Samira said, before he could answer. 'We must return to our guesthouse. The others will be waiting. We're already late.' She headed to the cashier's window to pay for her purchase.

Girnar waited until she was out of earshot. 'Samira's part of my group, that's all,' he said to Mrs Morrison, hoping she would understand they weren't a couple. Mrs Morrison shrugged. 'What about tomorrow?' he said, trying to sound casual. 'I'm free tomorrow.'

'Tomorrow I have an appointment,' she said. 'I'm going to the burning ghats early in the morning for an interview.'

'The burning ghats!' he said. 'Do you know what happens there?' Before Mrs Morrison could reply, Girnar launched into a description of Hindu cremation rites. She listened attentively and he knew she was impressed with his knowledge. 'I can come with you tomorrow,' he said.

After a brief hesitation, she said, 'Okay. You could be my translator. My Hindi is not very good.' She laughed, 'In fact it's dreadful. I only know a few phrases.' They arranged to meet at her hotel the next morning. 'Until tomorrow,'

Mrs Morrison said, and held out her hand. As he shook it, Girnar felt as though she was sealing a business deal with him and he felt a little let down.

As soon as he was out of the shop, Samira said, 'Professor-ji, how do you know that foreign woman?'

'Mrs Morrison?' he said. 'We met some time back.' The footpath was crowded with people and Samira didn't notice the broad smile on Girnar's face or the slight jump in his step.

~

That evening after dinner the group sat around the dining table in the courtyard. Everyone was tired but no one wanted the day to end. Jadu, the servant, and two others from the kitchen sat on their haunches in the corner smoking beedis. Fluorescent tubes lit up the courtyard. From outside the compound wall came the muffled twang of film music and once in a while the jangle of a rickshaw careening down the lane. Girnar looked around at the group. He planned to begin writing his book tonight. He must be disciplined and set a good pace from the start. He leaned back in his chair and studied the neem tree in the courtyard. His bandaged head had not bothered him all day, but now he fished in his shirt pocket for the medicine the doctor at the clinic had given him. The pills were in his room, and he felt irritated for not having them handy. He folded his arms across his chest and listened to the babble at the table for a few more minutes before retreating to his room, pleading a growing headache and touching the bandage. They sympathized and wished him a good night of sleep.

In his room he peeled two pills from the sheaf and swallowed them without water. Jadu had got him four exercise books and a pen. The books were thin, a hundred pages each, and the pen of poor quality, but he was overcome with childish excitement. He arranged the exercise books in a stack on the sewing machine and scribbled a few curly dashes on the cover to test the pen. Tossing his shirt on a chair, he paced the room.

~

Thousands of years ago, Shiva and Parvati had met at Mount Kailash. If Girnar were writing a mythological novel, it would be easy to dramatize the courtship of Shiva and Parvati. This was how he imagined it: Shiva, sitting in the lotus position with eyes closed, meditating. One morning when a big sun is rising in the cold Himalayan sky, the youthful Parvati comes before Shiva. Parvati's sari is tied low on her hips, the gossamer fabric clinging to her thighs; her earlobes are dabbed with sandalwood oil and white jasmines decorate her hair. A tight blouse accentuates her bosom, and the pendant of an exquisite necklace is nestled just so in the shadowy space between her breasts. Parvati starts singing and calling Shiva's name, but to no avail. She starts dancing, swinging her hips and thrusting her breasts with such provocation that even the sun is embarrassed and slips behind a cloud. After many hours, when the distracted Shiva finally opens his eyes, Parvati demurely averts her gaze. It is a little gesture—the flutter of eyelashes with the slight downward movement of her neck—but it is enough. The course of a major world religion is forever altered. Shiva's trident slips from his hand, his skin tingles in delight. Meditation, now, is out of the question. They are married immediately. The ceremony is a simple affair, but the night of their consummation…Who can imagine the lovemaking of the gods?...The depth of emotion, the acrobatic positions, the protracted moment of ecstasy, the entire Mount Kailash trembling and heaving.

Girnar pulled the chair close to the sewing machine and sat down. Envisioning the congress of Shiva and Parvati would get him nowhere. His gaze drifted to the open window. Along with the glow of lights from the courtyard came the pilgrims' voices. He had undertaken to write *their* stories, not a bawdy mythological novel. There was no time to waste. Tomorrow he must rise early to accompany Mrs Morrison to the burning ghats. He opened the book, uncapped the pen, and started writing.

3

On the way to Mrs Morrison's hotel, Girnar longed for a cup of tea to shake off his tiredness. A few roadside stalls were already open for business, but he didn't want to be late. Despite having stayed up past midnight, he had leapt out of bed with the first ring of the alarm clock. He had bathed, dressed, and left the guesthouse before any of his companions were up.

The bandage on his head felt damp and scratchy on one side. A few schoolchildren hurried past as he approached the hotel. It was a three-storeyed structure at the end of a long row of shorter buildings. The third floor of the hotel, probably a recent addition, was newly painted. There was a small garden in front with a statue in the centre. Girnar stopped for a moment to adjust his shirt. There was no reason for him to be nervous about meeting Mrs Morrison. At the college in Ahmedabad, they sometimes had foreign visitors, and the principal, a quiet bookish man he admired, always entrusted him with the task of showing them the campus. 'They will want to know about Hinduism,' the principal would say. 'Could you kindly keep them occupied for the afternoon?' Over the years, Girnar had learned to converse easily with Americans and Europeans as he escorted them through the seven interconnected Gothic-style buildings of the college.

Once he was invited to an academic conference at the Oriental Studies Centre in London, but when he approached the principal for travel funds, the man crossed his arms over his chest and in a tone Girnar had never thought him capable of, informed Girnar that he was heading an Indian institution of higher learning, not the World Bank. Word of his extravagant request got around the staff room and although no one said anything to his face, he knew they were sniggering and making fun of him.

He kept out of the principal's sight as well as the staff room for a while. His anger drove him to the city's passport office, where he picked up an application and at a small studio nearby got passport photos made. He started dreaming of a job at a foreign university, in England or America, where Hindu mythology would be a foreign subject and the pay in foreign money. But he never filled out the passport application and stashed it along with the photos in the lower drawer of his desk at home.

In the garden outside Mrs Morrison's hotel he sat on a ledge, perching at the edge so as not to wrinkle his pants or get them dusty. The lane was silent in the early morning sunlight, picturesque almost with the old buildings, the shuttered shops, the rows of drying clothes hanging overhead, and it was hard to imagine the cycle-rickshaws, pedestrians and stray cows soon to populate the scene.

A uniformed groundskeeper appeared from a side door of the hotel. After raising his hand in a casual salute to Girnar, he began sweeping the short walkway, stooping over the broom, making slow, deliberate arcs. When he was done sweeping, he threw the broom in the grass and paused under the statue to light up a beedi. Girnar hadn't paid much attention to the statue, but now he noticed it was a tall marble figure and seemed out of place in the small garden. But then, so many things in India were out of place.

Mrs Morrison emerged from the front door in a white salwar kameez. Forgetting his tiredness, he stood up briskly. The groundskeeper eyed Girnar curiously and although he felt slightly awkward at this scrutiny, he didn't let it dampen his mood. Mrs Morrison greeted him with a smile and after exchanging pleasantries they set off for the road leading to the burning ghats.

The area around the hotel had been quiet, but as they approached the main road there were small bands of people milling about. The alleys were lined with incense shops and vendors hawking marigold wreaths and ritual oils. Red and yellow pennants crisscrossed above, flapping with the occasional breeze.

'How was your visit to the old city yesterday?' he said.

She nodded enthusiastically. 'You should have come with me,' she said. 'It was incredible. There was a parade of elephants. I've never seen anything like it.'

When he was young, he had ridden an elephant in Jaipur. He remembered the colourful palanquin, the queue of squealing children, and his father snapping photos with his old Pentax. It seemed banal to describe this long ago memory to Mrs Morrison. Besides, what had impressed him most at the time were the huge globs of dung plopping from the animal's rump.

'One of the elephants broke off from the herd,' Mrs Morrison said, 'and the mahout started shouting like a madman. It was a sight to see, a big elephant trumpeting through the crowded lanes.'

'Did he catch his elephant?'

'Yes,' she said, laughing. 'I took some photos. The chalk designs on the elephants are so artful.'

'Art in motion!' he said.

Foreigners in Benares were not uncommon, but as they walked through the lanes, he noticed several people staring openly at Mrs Morrison. She seemed used to it and dismissed the beggars with a sympathetic but determined shake of her head. He wondered how her husband could have allowed her to travel here alone. Although she was not stylish, she was not unattractive. Her large expressive eyes reminded him of seashells. He grew self-conscious walking beside her, thinking people who looked at them probably thought they were a couple.

As they approached the burning ghats, the lane suddenly filled with people carrying a bier with a dead body to the river. A few in front played hand cymbals and chanted prayers. Girnar and Mrs Morrison stepped aside as the body, draped with a colourful sheet and covered with flowers, glided past them.

On the wide sand bank below the steps, several bodies were lined up for cremation, each surrounded by small groups of people. Priests officiated at some of the groups, performing the last rites. Logs of firewood lay here and there. A row of six or seven pyres blazed at one end, the bodies already obscured under the flaming tinder. Dozens of men squatted near the water as barbers shaved their heads in honour of the dead.

The Ganges pulsed silently. The dark grey water faded to light brown near the banks where sodden flower petals and half-cut coconuts lay trapped among the stones. Fields of tall grass stretched at the opposite shore, about two hundred metres away.

Asking directions from a few people, they found Ishwarnath, the chief priest. He was moustachioed, with dark skin and a thin stooped physique. His office was a ramshackle shed built of corrugated tin. There were a couple of cracked plastic chairs inside and an old padlocked trunk in the corner. Sand from outside had blown over the cement floor.

Ishwarnath offered them his good chairs, dusting them off with a large colourful cloth, not unlike the ones covering the bodies. From a wad in his shirt pocket he peeled a few rupees and sent his assistant, an impish boy of ten or twelve, to fetch tea for his guests. Gesturing to Girnar's bandage, he said, 'What happened?' When Girnar told him, he looked in the direction of the river and bowed his head.

They spoke in Hindi and Girnar translated for Mrs Morrison. Ishwarnath was angry about the electric crematorium built a few metres from the burning ghats. It was a small brick structure with two furnaces, and white tiles on the floor, 'like a bathroom,' he sneered. The rich politicians who lived in the British-style bungalows at Civil Lines were the perpetrators, he said. The electric cremation was cheaper and supposedly more efficient, but the modern contraption made a mockery of death. '*We* are performing ancient rituals,' he said, raising his chin, 'Without these rituals how can the soul ascend to heaven?' He coughed incessantly as he spoke, every once in a while rising from his chair to spit outside.

Mrs Morrison, who was writing in her notebook, stopped and asked whether Ishwarnath had seen a doctor about his cough.

'Of course, many times,' he said, waving a hand dismissively in the air. The doctor had prescribed two different tonics and a bottle of tablets. 'The medicines are expensive, but useless,' he said, shaking his head. The doctor had advised him not to work around the burning ghats; the smoke from the fires was aggravating his condition. 'The doctor was a fool. How can I give up my livelihood?' Ishwarnath said. 'Who will look after my family?' He braced himself as another fit of coughing took hold. As his cough subsided he leaned toward Girnar and said, 'Tell her not to write what I said about the doctor. He wasn't a bad man. He was only doing his job.'

Mrs Morrison looked down at her notes and nodded. She wanted to know how Ishwarnath dealt with being surrounded by death every day; did it not make him sad?

Ishwarnath smiled broadly. 'Once we are born, death is certain...Birth and death, these are two modes of being. It is the cycle of the cosmos. There is no cause for sadness.'

Mrs Morrison nodded uncertainly.

Ishwarnath asked if his name would appear in the story, and beamed in approval when Mrs Morrison said it would. He suggested she meet the politicians who had built the crematorium, he would be happy to supply their names. Could she meet them tomorrow? She could write about them, describe their evil practices, and that might force them to close down their operation.

Mrs Morrison said there was no time; she was leaving for Allahabad the next day.

'Allahabad?' Girnar said. 'We have chartered a bus. You can come with us!'

Ishwarnath touched Girnar's arm. 'Why won't she help me? If she talks to the politicians...'

Mrs Morrison shook her head emphatically. 'I cannot talk to the politicians. I'm leaving tomorrow. Besides, I'm not here to settle a fight.'

Ishwarnath sighed loudly and put his head in his hands.

Girnar gestured frantically at Mrs Morrison. 'You shouldn't refuse like that,' he said.

'What?' she said, scanning her notes and looking up, confused.

Girnar didn't know how to explain the formality to her. He lowered his voice. 'In India we say "yes" to everything. We say we will do it, even if we can't. It promotes hope.'

'I see,' she said, though he was not sure she did.

They left Ishwarnath's office and walked quietly up the steps that led into town. 'Thank you for coming with me,' she said as they climbed the rest of the steps. At the top, they stopped to catch their breaths. Behind them the smoke from the pyres rose like an apparition drifting over the river, and stretching before them stood the timeworn buildings and crowded lanes of Benares.

From her bag, Mrs Morrison brought out a guidebook and opened it to a page displaying a map of the city. She pointed to a red square on the map and said there was an art show at the exhibition grounds. Suddenly Girnar felt a sharp pain in his head. It lasted but a few seconds, starting from a concentrated point in the centre of his skull and radiating in a straight line to the wound on his forehead. Later, he would wonder if this was a premonitory sign of the dangerous event that took place that morning, but at the time, as soon as the pain subsided, he forgot about it.

A big white tent stood at the exhibition grounds. Large posters of gods and brightly coloured flags decorated the front. Music from loudspeakers—a shrill chorus of female voices—rang out in every direction; Mrs Morrison and Girnar heard the music even before seeing the tent.

Inside, after following a long corridor, they arrived in a large arena. Here, to his amazement, arranged in a series of life-size dioramas, were scenes from the *Ramayana*. The hero, Rama, in King Janaka's court, his hand drawing on his bow with tangible pressure; Bharata beseeching his mother to retract her selfish boon; Rama, Sita and Laxman exiled in the forest for fourteen years; Sita tempted by an innocent deer; Hanuman the monkey god, his tail ablaze, sent to rescue the abducted Sita; the furious battle with the demonic ten-headed Ravan; and Rama's glorious return to reclaim the kingdom. Some scenes were meticulously detailed and artistically rendered; others stylized, almost cartoonish.

Dozens of schoolchildren—girls and boys, ten or eleven years old, in maroon uniforms—spilled into the arena. They chattered excitedly as they went through the exhibit in single file, a few teachers minding them. An old man and woman who'd preceded them at the ticket booth sat on a bench sharing a snack from a brown paper bag. Mrs Morrison and Girnar were waiting to one side for the children to pass when a commotion startled them both. Outside, the loudspeakers cut off abruptly and instead of music they heard angry shouts. Several men sauntered into the arena, some with handkerchiefs tied on their heads, some shirtless and barefoot. Their faces bore hard expressions, and the way they were pacing told Girnar to avoid looking them in the eye.

The next instant the children were screaming, and Girnar

saw the men smashing the dioramas with sticks and axes. The children started running helter-skelter, their teachers flailing their arms and yelling, urging them to stay calm. Girnar saw Ravan's heads getting axed, Sita's body lashed with sticks, and Rama's throne knocked to pieces. 'Let's go!' he said to Mrs Morrison, who was grim-faced and poised to flee. The old couple on the bench sat in disbelief, watching the pandemonium, but unable to move, their snack spilling on the ground. Girnar shouted to them, 'Hey, come on.' He stopped to shake the old man's shoulders and they emerged from their shock and began making for an exit. Girnar saw clouds of smoke and thought the place was on fire, but it was dust and debris from broken plaster filling the air.

A mob had gathered outside. Mrs Morrison paused and looked back at Girnar. 'Whatever are all these people doing?' she said. 'Where are the police?'

Girnar saw the placards with provocative slogans and knew immediately that the altercation was caused by student groups. He'd read in the newspaper about the violence that had broken out on the university campus over students' demands to hold union elections. The protest had started as a peaceful demonstration at the campus gates but soon turned violent and spread to the entire campus, forcing the police to close down the university. Girnar glanced behind him at the faces of the rioters…their fury notwithstanding, how young most of them looked. He couldn't understand what had prompted them to bring their quarrel with university officials to an art show at the exhibition grounds. But now was not the time to try and make sense of political motives.

'Don't stop,' he said to Mrs Morrison. 'Just go!'

They raced out of the exhibition grounds. He found a rickshaw and they piled in, perspiring and panicked. 'Student riots,' he said to her. 'Students at Banaras Hindu University have been protesting for the past few weeks. They want proper elections for a student union instead of the university administration running their own polls.' She nodded nervously and kept looking over her shoulder. Barely five hundred metres from the exhibition grounds, it was as though nothing had happened—the footpaths were busy with people going about their day.

When they reached Mrs Morrison's hotel she invited him inside for tea. 'Or, we could have an early lunch, if it's ready,' she said, still a little breathless from all the excitement.

'Just tea, please,' he said, feeling suddenly shy.

~

That night in his room he sat on the chair near the sewing machine. He must ask Niranjan for a room with a proper desk at the next hotel. The four notebooks were tucked away at the bottom of his suitcase. Instead of sending Jadu, he had gone to the shop himself and bought a better pen. Now opening the first book, he stared at the empty page. He could write a story and weave in something about dioramas getting smashed by an angry mob. But politics was treacherous terrain for a writer.

He stood up and paced the room. He changed into his pajamas, then busied himself folding the dirty clothes and arranging them in the zippered compartment of his suitcase. He spent longer than usual brushing his teeth and rubbing his gums with the herbal tooth powder his mother made with a mortar and pestle at home. He had used the powder all his life and never had any cavities, and his teeth were straight, so it must be good. He stretched and yawned, rubbing his eyes. The mattress of the bed was hard and the pillow was thin, yet how inviting it looked now. But this was not the time to sleep and dream and bungle up his imagination. He was no ordinary writer; he was a writer with a mission. He sat down, took a few sips of water, and took up his pen.

4

Daylight nudged the windows of the small foyer of the guesthouse. It was nearly six o'clock and their luggage lay piled outside waiting to be loaded onto the bus expected to arrive at any minute. Girnar introduced Mrs Morrison to the group. Samira had already met her at the sari shop, but from Samira's cursory 'good morning' he could tell she wasn't pleased about Mrs Morrison travelling with them. The others stared openly, as though they'd never seen a foreign woman wearing a salwar kameez before, or maybe it was the white canvas shoes. He articulated the 'Missus'—but he knew some of them were wondering whether he liked her in 'that way'. Mrs Morrison offered to pay for her seat, but Niranjan refused. 'You can send us a copy of your magazine,' he said. The others nodded.

The bus roared through the lane and stopped at the front door. It was a brand new silver and blue air-conditioned bus with tinted windows. Everyone climbed aboard excitedly. Niranjan shouted instructions to the driver and his attendant as they loaded the luggage. The driver, whose name was Krishnan, a tall strapping fellow with curly grey hair, wore a driver's uniform, blue long pants and a silver-grey shirt that matched the colours of the bus. His assistant, Arjunesh, wore a bright yellow shirt, the collar turned rakishly up, the buttons open at the chest. The lane was narrow, so Krishnan edged the bus in reverse all the way to the main road with Arjunesh running alongside, yelling and banging on the side. Girnar chuckled to himself at the irony of their names—in the Bhagvadgita, Arjuna was the warrior prince and Krishna his divine charioteer.

In the seat next to Mrs Morrison, Girnar stretched his legs in the aisle.

'Is your head better?' she said. 'The bandage looks different.'

The night before, he had unwrapped the original bandage and, as he leaned over the sink to inspect the wound in the mirror, he was horrified. The lesion, horizontal and two inches long, was in the exact centre of his forehead. With a wad of wet cotton he tried to dab off the purple Mercurochrome, but it stung too much and after a few pats, he tossed the wad in the trash pail under the sink. The stitches were a nasty grey-green colour, and the skin around the wound grey and swollen. Even after everything healed, there would be a big scar. He decided to wear a hat, or a turban, or grow his hair and comb it over his forehead, anything to hide this new deformity. He leaned closer to the mirror and noticed that the gash on his forehead was slightly curved, and there was another crescent-shaped laceration below the puffy skin. The whole wound resembled an eye—in fact, it looked like Shiva's third eye. A wave of pride washed over him as he stepped back from the mirror. The eye on Shiva's forehead was a symbol of knowledge, of a higher consciousness, capable of emanating beams of fire to destroy evil. It suddenly occurred to Girnar that the gash on his forehead was no ordinary wound. It was a mark of the divine.

'My head is much improved,' he said to Mrs Morrison, touching his forehead reverentially. 'This is a new bandage and it's not as tight as the previous one.'

'Do you have a family? A wife?' she asked.

He wasn't surprised by the question. She smiled as he described his parents and their old-fashioned ways. She was impressed he had been teaching for almost twenty years, and he couldn't help boasting a little as he spoke about his classes and his small, earnest band of students.

When he confessed his position at the college might soon disappear because of changing demands in education, she was surprised. 'Hindu mythology is not popular in India?' she said.

Some years ago, in an effort to boost enrolment, he had proposed teaching a course on the *Kama Sutra* with a weeklong field trip to the Khajuraho Temples at the end of the term. He put a great deal of effort into writing the course description, carefully explaining that the *Kama Sutra* was not merely a sex manual but rather a treatise on virtuous living, material prosperity, sensual pleasure, and enlightenment. The goal of his course was to study the *interconnections* between eroticism and spirituality. But everything at the college had to be approved by the ministry of education. His course was roundly rejected, and deemed 'careless', 'scandalous', and 'certain to promote loose morals'.

'My daughter is seventeen,' she said. 'She's at Seven Oaks, it's a boarding school outside London. Next year she'll go to university.' She searched in her purse and pulled out a leather case that opened like a card and revealed her daughter's photo. 'That's Adela,' she said, holding out a photo of a smiling girl with shoulder-length hair, in a red dress.

'She is good-looking,' he said.

Mrs Morrison studied the photograph.

'And your husband?' he asked.

Her face tightened. 'It was not an easy marriage. We were both too young when we married. We were separated when he died three years ago.'

Girnar gasped. 'I'm sorry,' he said, under his breath. Should he ask how he had died? He had never imagined her without a husband. In the long silence that followed, he looked down at his hands, absently clasping and unclasping his fingers, wondering if Mrs Morrison and he were meant for each other. Why else had he run into her in Benares in the middle of the night? Not only would he have a wife, but a daughter as well—a ready-made family. He glanced at her profile. Her face was fair and smooth and exotic. His parents would be sceptical about him marrying a foreign woman, and he was sure they would try to talk him out of it. But he would explain how 'Indian' she really was. She was already used to wearing Indian clothes, even though she used the dupatta as a belt instead of draping it modestly over her shoulders. Besides, he could easily coax her into wearing a sari when he introduced her to his parents. By far the best thing about Mrs Morrison was that she was a writer. They could be a genuine team. He imagined them sitting at their desks each night, hurrying to finish their work, and then falling into bed...

Mrs Morrison stared at him for a moment. She closed the leather photo case hurriedly and slipped it into her purse.

Feeling embarrassed and useless, regretting his indulgent thoughts, he turned to the window. The bus had just cleared the city limits and they were travelling fast on the open road. 'This is all sacred ground,' he said, gesturing with one hand to the fields outside. 'This is where the events of the *Ramayana* took place...'

Mrs Morrison listened intently, taking notes as he spoke.

'...more than two thousand years ago.'

She glanced out the bus window. A broken pillar from a temple with images of Rama and Sita seated on a throne lay on the side of the road, without context. Flowers were strewn at its base, a coconut balanced near Sita's lap. 'It seems as though they took place only yesterday,' she said.

'Ours is an oral culture,' he said. 'You must understand this. The stories of the *Ramayana* are repeated day after day in Hindu households. People identify with the heroes, the actual time and year are less important.'

'I see,' she said, but as he watched her writing in her notebook, he doubted she understood the extent to which myths had shaped India. She kept writing and glancing out the window and he studied her profile. Her handwriting was small and neat, almost like print, the sentences running slightly uphill on the unlined page. When the time came to tell his mother about Mrs Morrison, he would stress the fact that she was born in India.

~

They stopped outside Mirzapur for breakfast. The restaurant, a large square building across the road from the riverbank, was surrounded by big trees. Several cars and another tour bus were parked in a clearing. While Niranjan went in to see about tables for their group, and the others waited on the verandah, Mrs Morrison and Girnar wandered outside.

Opposite the restaurant, a small circular building with a

tiled roof turned out to be a carpet-weaving factory. Girnar asked the watchman at the gate if they could walk to the back of the compound to see the river.

The watchman eyed his bandage and squinted at Mrs Morrison. 'Government people are not allowed inside the gate,' he said offhandedly.

'We're not government people,' Girnar said, slipping him a few rupees.

They strolled down the narrow dirt path leading to the back, Girnar a few paces ahead of Mrs Morrison. In places, the grass around the path was almost waist-high. Birds flitted in the dense branches overhead.

Mrs Morrison told him she had attended a conference of Freshwater Ecosystems in Delhi and had met the top officials. 'The factories along the Ganges are ordered to treat their wastewater before dumping it into the river,' she said, 'but some of them simply ignore the ordinance.'

Girnar stopped and pointed to a narrow canal. 'Is that what you're referring to?' Barely visible behind a clump of hedges, a drainpipe from the factory secreted a thick dark-green liquid into the river.

She let out a sad groan and pulled out her camera.

Girnar pointed to the building behind them. 'Small factories like this one can't afford to invest in environmental protection.'

'I know,' she said, aiming the camera and clicking. 'The government is going to help them.'

Girnar laughed. 'What a thing to assume in India,' he said.

'And look there,' she said, gesturing downstream where dozens of children frolicked in the polluted water and nearby a man performed his ablutions, arms skyward. Adjusting the lens, she took more photos.

Girnar laughed again and said, 'King Sagara's sixty thousand sons were saved when the Ganges came down to earth.'

'What?'

'Nothing,' he said, kicking a stone on the path. 'Only another myth.' He knew the pollution of the Ganges was a serious issue, but he hadn't given it much thought. 'Mrs Morrison,' he said, 'because of you, and the article you write, the Ganges will soon be clean.'

'You're being sarcastic?' There was an expression bordering on anger on her face as she put away the camera. They stood in silence for a few moments, looking at the river. Suddenly she burst out, 'Don't you understand what's happening to your river? Don't you care? You people think flowers and coconuts will balance everything.'

He hadn't meant to be sarcastic; if anything, he had meant it as a light-hearted compliment. 'Mrs Morrison, I'm sorry...'

She turned and marched back up the path ahead of him. In the restaurant, after ordering breakfast, she sat with the group, talking with the others, refusing to look at him.

On the bus, he apologized again. As he watched her write in her notebook, he decided to contact the ministry of ecosystems in Delhi and get himself invited to their meetings. He could start an organization to save the river: *Save Goddess Ganges*. He would refer to it by the acronym SGG. It might grow to become an all-Asia organization; there were so many rivers in Asia that needed to be rescued—the Yangtze, Mekong, Tigris, and Euphrates. And, why stop at Asia, he could lead a worldwide project—the Volga, Rhine, Danube, Nile, Congo, Mississippi, Amazon—*Save the World's Rivers*. SWR. Surely that would impress Mrs Morrison.

~

They reached Allahabad in the afternoon. Mrs Morrison went off to stay at the home of a business associate. 'See you later,' she said to Girnar, waving from the taxi. Where? When? he wanted to ask, but he was left standing on the footpath watching the back of her head as the taxi disappeared into a dusty blare of traffic.

He ate lunch with his group, but while everyone around him chatted, he sat quietly, keeping his disappointment to himself, fearing he might never see her again. *Because of you, the Ganges will soon be clean*—if only he had not said that.

After lunch he set off with the others to see the confluence of the Ganges and the Yamuna. The third river, the Saraswati, was invisible, but people still believed in her ancient spirit. Scores of boats with colourful flags waited near the shore to ferry people to the auspicious site.

He lifted his face to the wind as they chugged along in a large, new-looking boat. The air carried a whiff of petrol and the din of jubilant voices. White herons floated overhead. In the distance he could see the curve of the Yamuna, a long ribbon eager to merge with the Ganges. The waters ran pristine in every direction, no empty plastic bottles and sodden cigarette boxes, not even scraps of flowers floating on the surface, and no charred corpses.

Approaching the confluence, the current slowed the boat and they drifted quietly. It was all serenity. The boatwallah announced, '*Ganga Mata ki jai, Yamuna Mata ki jai. Saraswati Mata ki jai.*' Hail to the three goddesses.

Girnar leaned over and trailed his fingers in the water.

'Get your hand out!' the boatwallah yelled. 'Gharial. Look there.'

Girnar knew about gharials, the crocodiles of the Ganges. They ate fish and frogs, but still, they might mistake his hand for a juicy fish. He squinted towards the shore where the boatwallah pointed. He couldn't see any gharials, but took his hand out of the water.

After the boat ride, he strolled the Kumbh festival grounds with his group. He kept looking for Mrs Morrison, expecting to see her at every turn. He wandered in and out of shops, hoping to find her interviewing another shopkeeper. The afternoon sun beat down sternly, dispelling the prospect of any respite from the meagre breeze.

At the gates of a large temple, as they stood in queue to give their sandals to an attendant, he casually brought up the Ganges and the topic of pollution with Samira.

'Professor-ji,' Samira eyed him cautiously. 'It's like this: in India we sweep our own houses and push the dirt to the road. No one takes responsibility for the dirt on the road. The same is true with the river. People will go on throwing things into the water because they believe the gods will take care of the river. There's nothing you or I, or your foreign Mrs Morrison can do about it.'

He resented the dash of contempt in the way she said 'Mrs Morrison.'

'Ancient beliefs can accommodate modern science,' Girnar said, resentment at his nation's collective ignorance in his voice. 'India's achievements are a result of...'

'India's achievements!' Samira scoffed. 'We think too much of ourselves, that's the problem. Three thousand years ago we invented the zero, the very basis of modern mathematics. We got a pat on the back from Albert Einstein. A great feat: discovery of the void. What have we achieved since then? Zero.' Leaning towards his face, she put her thumb and index finger together. 'Nothing.'

He was taken aback but also mildly impressed by her vehemence. As they entered the temple compound, he stopped at the moneychangers who sat on the ground with small mountains of coins in front of them. The walkway to the temple was lined with beggars. After changing some notes, he dropped alms in a few of the old metal begging bowls. He was used to seeing poverty, but suddenly at the back of his mind, a tiny fear started growing and taking root. The beggars would be here forever, even if their alms bowls overflowed. The thought filled him with anxiety, like a newly discovered fear. Samira's pessimism about India's achievements sat like a dull weight on his shoulders. The temple bells announced the start of the puja. Moving quickly to catch a place at the front of the crowd, he tried to match his stride to the clanging bells.

Behind the temple, at the ghats, he sat on the steps while the others bathed in the river. He didn't want to risk getting his bandage wet, or falling in. Left on the steps to mind the group's belongings, he nudged everything into a neat pile and settled down.

With the temple domes reflecting the sinking sun's light, he watched a group of Brahmins rubbing oil and sandalwood paste on their arms and chests, chanting verses in Sanskrit as they performed this ritual. He listened to their recitation and realized the pilgrimage was drawing him in. At the outset he had remained somewhat dispassionate, the holy cities along the river representing nothing more than places to pass through until he returned home, to resume his old routine at the college. But now, he was beginning to understand the transformative power of each place. Perhaps his nightly labour of writing contributed to this sense of heightened awareness.

Something curious had happened the night before. The moment he started writing, the story simply unfurled in his head. He never paused to search for a word or a phrase, or to think if something was plausible. He never went back over a sentence or crossed out a paragraph. It seemed as though a quiet voice was dictating the story and he was merely writing it down. The voice spoke clearly and with authority. If it was a long word or a complicated sentence, the voice slowed and kept pace with his pen. If he stopped to rest his hand or take a few sips of water, the voice stopped too. At first he thought a prolific muse had taken up a perch at his shoulder, but gradually he sensed the voice and he were one, all his years of reading, writing, and teaching merging as a kaleidoscopic carousel through which the voice was speaking.

~

That evening he ate with the pilgrims in the dining room of the Sangam Hotel. It was an old colonial-style room with marble floors and polished furniture. Dinner—mulligatawny soup, bread rolls, vegetables au gratin, and fruit custard—was served in fine porcelain dishes. At the end of the meal, everyone complimented Niranjan for booking such a fine hotel. The atmosphere of the dining room put Girnar in a good mood and he found himself joking and laughing with his companions.

Sangam Hotel sat on a hill above the bazaar and from certain rooms there was a view of the river. Girnar's room was at the back of the building and there was no view of anything. Its single, small window was set high on the wall. But his heart leapt at the big wooden desk. The legs and sides were elaborately carved and the writing surface was covered in leather with tooled brass edging. There was even a desk lamp—click-click—he smiled at the bright pool of light. He sat in the chair, and, pressing his back into it, noted the generous padding. Tonight he would write in luxury.

5

Girnar awoke with a start. A loud knocking on the door was followed by a voice shouting his name. From the window near the ceiling a bright beam of sunlight pierced the room. He stared at the fan, whirring at full speed, and the tiny dust particles floating upward into random motes. He was stretched out on the bed, still in yesterday's clothes. Heaviness nagged his head, his right thumb and index finger felt raw and blistered. His gaze wandered uncertainly over the furnishings. The desk lamp was on, his notebooks were scattered on the table, the chair had toppled over, and his pen was on the floor.

He had no memory of when he had gotten up from the desk, but now as his feet found the small carpet by the bed, the story he had written last night swirled in his head. 'One minute!' he shouted, as the knocking on the door persisted. He straightened the chair, shoved the pen and notebooks into a drawer, and stumbled to the door.

Niranjan barged into the room. For a second Girnar thought Niranjan had materialized from the pages of his story. 'What happened to you?' Niranjan said. 'You didn't come for breakfast, and now it's past lunch-time!' He gestured to his head, 'What happened to the bandage?'

Girnar glanced in the mirror above the bureau. The

bandage was a ragtag heap on his head, one straggly end hanging on his shoulder.

'What is wrong with you?' Niranjan said, irritated. 'Don't just stand there, get ready and go downstairs.' He closed the door, then poked his head back in. 'Your friend, Mrs Morrison, is here to see you.'

For a moment Girnar stood staring at the closed door. Mrs Morrison was here to see him! He sprung into action. 'Tell her I'll be down in ten minutes,' he called loudly, hoping Niranjan could hear him, as he rummaged in his suitcase for a clean set of clothes and then rushed to shave and bathe.

When he went downstairs, he found Mrs Morrison sitting on a sofa in the small lobby bar near the reception desk, sipping a lemon soda. 'I stopped by to say hello,' she said.

'Well, then, hello,' he said, trying to sound casual, and lowered himself into a chair opposite her.

'I ordered for you. Here—' She poured the second bottle of lemon soda into a glass.

'Thank you,' he said, accepting the glass. 'You're having a pleasant time in Allahabad?' He hated how dull and formal he sounded. He glanced around the lobby, which was empty except for a waiter clearing another table and a clerk at the reception desk talking on the phone.

'Yes. I spent the better part of the morning organizing my notes and then started writing my article, which is proving to be a challenge even though I have some interesting material from the interviews so far. And you, what have you been doing?'

He had been in bed all morning, not in restful sleep

but in some sort of thick stupor during which it seemed as though he was writing an endless string of random words and reading them aloud to himself. Thinking about this now, he panicked a little, and wondered if he was having some sort of nervous breakdown; perhaps all this writing had not been good for his head injury.

'I've been thinking,' he said, as the loose strand of an idea started to take hold. 'I've been thinking about water pollution.'

She eyed him sceptically.

He finished the lemon soda, set the glass down, and cleared his throat. 'What you were saying the other day about the ministry of ecology in Delhi…'

'It's called, ministry of freshwater ecosystems.'

'I'm interested in the government ordinance,' he said. 'I want to get involved in cleaning the river. I've been thinking about this rather seriously…'

'Really? Why? You think it has some connection to Hindu mythology? Well, let me tell you…'

'Yes, exactly!' he said. 'This is India, Mrs Morrison. And in India, everything is connected to Hindu mythology.' He finished his drink and returned the glass to the tray with a flourish. 'Please,' he said, sitting up straighter and looking directly at her with as much seriousness as he could muster. 'Please tell me what you know about the government ordinance.'

'Okay, okay,' she said, laughing easily.

She explained that close to a billion litres of industrial sewage flowed into the Ganges each year. The government had set up sewage treatment plants, but the electricity supply was unreliable, especially during the monsoons.

The new 'Ganges Campaign' levied high fines on factories that dumped untreated waste, but there were issues of mismanagement and corruption. Human and animal deaths caused by waterborne diseases were rampant.

'Scientists and engineers have stepped in too,' she said. 'At some points along the river the pathogen count has reached one hundred and fifty million bacteria per one hundred millimetres of water, which is three hundred thousand times more than the accepted level.'

He was inspired by her knowledge, the way she quoted facts and figures.

She explained that an American scientist had developed a water oxidation system that involved storing sewage in a series of ponds. Algae and bacteria were added to the ponds to break down the waste and purify the water.

Girnar imagined the stagnant ponds becoming breeding grounds for mosquitoes, but didn't voice this objection.

'Pollution of the Ganges is a sad, maddening problem,' she said, passionately. 'And, it's not just industrial pollution…'

'I know,' he said, recalling the remains of bodies and animal carcasses floating in the river.

'It's the eternal contradiction,' she said. 'The ancient and modern, religion and science.'

'I don't see any contradiction,' he said.

'No?' She leaned back in the sofa and crossed her arms. 'Tell me, Professor, what do you see?'

'There is no contradiction,' he said evenly. 'In fact, Hindu mythology can be invoked and channelled to create ecological awareness in India. The Ganges will always be sacred and Hindus will always go to her banks seeking salvation. But the stories of the gods have to be used more explicitly to generate a new attitude towards the environment.' Mrs Morrison was regarding him intently. He was surprised at himself for sounding so logical. 'What we need is large-scale national awareness as well as a way to empower local communities,' he added. She nodded, admiringly. 'I intend to launch a new campaign, Mrs Morrison. I believe my knowledge of mythology could save the river.'

'I see,' she said, her face bright and excited.

'We are all part of the river,' he continued, 'and we must realize that saving the river is really about saving ourselves. The Ganges isn't just a body of flowing water. She's a living, breathing goddess that's part of us.'

'Yes, yes, I fully agree,' she said. 'An approach that combines science and mythology, it's an excellent idea.'

As she launched into a discussion of biodiversity and water management, he listened closely, overwhelmed by how much and how quickly he had risen in her estimation.

6

Niranjan shouted, glancing at his watch, 'We can't wait for her! It is seven hundred kilometres to Haridwar. We must leave now.' Girnar paced the road looking for Mrs Morrison's taxi. The morning was dark and the road was empty. The group's luggage was loaded, everyone else had climbed aboard, and the motor was idling noisily. Niranjan, on the steps of the bus, was holding the door open.

Girnar walked slowly back to the bus. Now he would never see her again. What about the river, and the dozens of questions he had planned to ask her?

'Hurry up,' Niranjan said.

He begged Niranjan to wait for Mrs Morrison, something may have happened, she was a foreigner in their country and they couldn't leave her stranded like that. 'She's an old family friend,' he pleaded.

'Okay,' Niranjan shrugged. 'Five more minutes.'

The minutes ticked by. Girnar told Niranjan to go ahead with the group; he would wait for Mrs Morrison and they would find their way to Haridwar. Niranjan was reluctant, but finally agreed and as Girnar stood on the footpath watching the bus drive off, he felt both worried and irritated.

Mrs Morrison arrived ten minutes later. Her taxi had broken down and she'd walked for some time before finding an auto-rickshaw. 'The bus?' she said, stepping out of the rickshaw, 'Where are the others?'

Girnar gestured to the rickshawallah to wait.

When she learned the group had already left, she sighed loudly. 'You stayed back for me?' She put a hand on his arm and Girnar held his breath for a moment, thrilling at her touch. 'Thank you,' she said, 'but you could have gone on with them. I'm perfectly capable of travelling on my own.'

'Bus depot,' he said to the rickshawallah as he climbed in beside Mrs Morrison. 'We'll catch a public bus to Haridwar,' he said to her.

The bus depot was a large breezy area with a metal roof. Despite the early hour it was crowded with passengers and luggage. There was no direct bus to Haridwar, but they could go to Kanpur and catch another bus from there.

The bus to Kanpur was late. Girnar grew frustrated. 'Nothing in India ever runs on time,' he said, marching back from the ticket window where he had inquired about the bus for the third time. Mrs Morrison was unfazed, content to wait patiently on a bench amid the continual stares of people and the insistent waves of vendors hawking cigarettes, food, and tabloids. Now that they were to stop in Kanpur, she wanted to visit a tannery. She produced a name and address from her notebook. 'Then it all worked out for the best,' he said, trying to sound cheerful.

The bus, painted with colourful pictures of gods and birds, rolled into the station more than an hour late. Mrs Morrison's luggage, which was only a small suitcase and a lightweight bedding-roll, was hoisted onto the top by three coolies amid much deliberation and yelling. The bus was overbooked with a wedding party, but because Mrs Morrison was a foreigner, they were allowed in the reserved, first class seats, sectioned off by a string of plastic flowers in the front two rows behind the driver. Women in bright saris and big nose-rings and men in colourful vests and turbans filled the seats behind them.

As the bus rattled out of Allahabad and gained speed on the two-lane highway, the wedding party broke into song. Soon they were stomping and clapping, a few of them dancing in the aisle. Mrs Morrison looked on amusedly. As she turned and clicked a few photos, the dancers grew more enthusiastic, posing and encouraging her to take more pictures. Girnar wished the racket would stop. After a while the revellers grew tired, and a lull settled over the bus.

Wind whipping through the bus from the open windows brought with it dust and grime. The road was lined with fields of wheat and melons, and patches of wasteland where nothing grew. Old settlements of mud houses sat precariously on the riverbank.

'What you said the other day,' Mrs Morrison said, 'that in India one must say "yes" to everything, not refuse anyone…what were your words? "It promotes hope".'

He nodded.

'I've been thinking about it,' she said, pushing back her disarrayed hair.

'Really?' It was nothing he had expected her to consider seriously.

'What happens when the promise is not carried through?' she said. 'Does it not breed disappointment and frustration?'

He smiled broadly. 'It depends…'

'What's wrong with honesty?' she said. 'Why not simplify things? Say "yes" if you can do it, and "no" if you can't. That way you avoid bitterness in the future.'

He stared at her for a few moments. How to explain the nuances of the Indian psyche? 'The moment you refuse,' he said finally, watching as she opened her notebook to a clean page, 'the moment you refuse, bitterness beats in the heart of the person.' He looked over her shoulder at the page. He should say something profound since she was taking down what he said. 'The present moment is the most important,' he said quietly. 'God is here and everything is possible.'

She looked directly into his eyes, and sighed slowly. After clicking the pen a few times, she slid it into a leather hook on the notebook's cover and put everything away.

~

It was past lunchtime when the bus arrived at Kanpur. The connecting bus to Haridwar had already left and the next bus wasn't until tomorrow. Girnar groaned loudly, stomping his feet in irritation. Mrs Morrison seemed to take the delay in her stride. 'Oh, what a pity,' was all she remarked, and Girnar couldn't understand how she could be so calm, especially since he'd heard Americans and Europeans were punctual people and everything in their countries always ran on time.

They deliberated about spending the night in Kanpur and Girnar looked around for a Tourist Desk to ask about hotels.

'Wait,' Mrs Morrison said, 'What about hiring a taxi? Or, could we take a train?'

'Yes, I'm sure there's a train to Haridwar,' Girnar said. 'Let's hope we can get tickets.'

They walked to the train station, a short distance away, a coolie following with her luggage. After they had bought their tickets and deposited the luggage in the ladies' waiting room, they found a small restaurant near the station. Inside, a sign warned: *Meat, Eggs, Alcohol, Opium, not served or allowed on premises.* They looked over the sodden menu card. He chose the rice-curry plate. Mrs Morrison ordered tea, a bottle of Bisleri water and a packet of Glucose biscuits.

'We have several hours before the train,' she said. 'The tannery is on Station Road, so it can't be too far. Should we go?'

Girnar was tired and didn't feel like going anywhere. He wanted to buy a newspaper, find a bench on the platform, and wait for the train.

They took an auto-rickshaw, and travelled along a road beside the Ganges. The river limped through the barren marsh, a thin line meandering through small muddy pools. It was hard to imagine this was the mighty river. The landscape here was dry and colourless but for the occasional flash of a white egret. They bumped along the road, which narrowed and turned dustier, and cars and trucks gave way to bullock carts. Near the tannery the river recovered its strength and sped along.

The rickshawallah, a garrulous man in an orange shirt, asked why they were going to the tannery. It wasn't such a nice place, he said. They should see the Baradevi temple, which was the oldest temple in Kanpur, or, the Gora Kabristan, a British graveyard. When Girnar explained Mrs Morrison was writing about the river, he said, 'Goddess Ganga is a restless one.'

'Restless?' Girnar said.

'This road used to be there,' he said, pointing to a place about twenty metres to the right where the river made a slight bend. 'Who knows where she will go next.'

Girnar gazed out and imagined the river prowling over the land, shifting course at will. He pictured Goddess Ganga sitting up and moving her limbs, her eyes roving the tired landscape as she arched this way and that, testing her strength. The image of a restless goddess filled him with worry.

~

The tannery was a series of large sheds in the middle of a huge compound. The owner, Lal Prasad, a bulky man with cropped curly hair, did not offer tea. They sat in rattan chairs on the verandah of his house at the far end of the compound overlooking the river. He addressed himself exclusively to Girnar. Mrs Morrison inched her chair forward, but he still ignored her. Kanpur was full of leather industries, he said, but his was the oldest. It was set up by the British two hundred years ago for manufacturing boots and saddles. Lal Prasad spoke in a flat, matter-of-fact voice, as though he gave this speech dozens of times a day. Girnar tried to detect some friendliness on his face.

Lal Prasad bemoaned the demise of British rule in India. 'In 1843, the British built the first canal on the Upper Ganges that branched off from Haridwar. It was an incredible engineering feat at the time. But the Brahmins protested; they claimed the steel sluices would pollute the Ganges water.' Lal Prasad stopped and looked at Girnar accusingly, as though he had conspired with the Brahmins. 'No dam was built,' he continued, 'and the canal ran dry when the water level dropped.'

Mrs Morrison fidgeted with her notebook. 'I assume, sir,' she finally interrupted, 'that the waste matter at this tannery is sent to a pumping station?'

Lal Prasad's eyes turned flinty and for the first time he showed emotion. 'Do you think we dump raw effluent directly into the river?'

'The high levels of contaminants in the water,' she continued, 'are known to cause skin diseases and hepatitis and amoebic dysentery. I'm sure you are…'

Lal Prasad stood up abruptly. 'It is a hot day, I'll order some cold drinks,' he said. 'Afterwards my assistant will show you the facility,' he added, and disappeared into the house.

Girnar stared at the river, flowing peacefully on its way. 'The water looks clean, no?'

Mrs Morrison shook her head as she wrote in her notebook. 'I have this odd feeling about him,' she said in a low voice.

'Really?'

'Several months ago a surveyor from a private environment company in Delhi was murdered here,' she said.

'What!'

'Not so loud,' she said, raising a finger to her lips.

'Murdered?' he whispered. 'Are you sure?'

'The police reported it as "an accident",' she said and kept writing.

He stared at her. He couldn't decide whether to take her seriously and be worried, or to adopt her nonchalant attitude. Did she think Lal Prasad was involved in the murder? And if so, why were they here, sitting on a murderer's verandah contemplating the river and listening to him drone on about the British in India?

The minutes ticked by but the cold drinks and the assistant that Lal Prasad had promised never materialized. Girnar was relieved; the drinks might be poisoned. Mrs Morrison suggested they take a look around the place on their own. He wanted to leave immediately. 'The train,' he said feebly.

On the wide brick pathway that led to the tannery, he quickened his steps and kept looking over his shoulder at Lal Prasad's house. It was a newly whitewashed two-storey structure with abundant pink and purple flowers spilling over the compound wall. Did Lal Prasad have a gun? In India gun ownership was illegal, but bribes could buy anything. Glancing at the second-storey window, he imagined a sinister figure taking aim, a bullet splitting his skull.

They entered a large courtyard where six big vats stood in the centre. Several workers scurried about; no one paid any attention to Mrs Morrison and Girnar.

'That's probably where the skins are cured,' Mrs Morrison said, pointing to the vats.

His heart beat madly. He imagined the poor surveyor 'accidentally' thrown into one of the vats, suffocating in the bleach and lye. Channels and gutters ran across the courtyard, some half-filled with dark water. If the victim had been knifed, his blood might have filled these gutters. His gaze fell on a pile of old drums stacked in the corner. He edged closer and peeked inside one that was half open. It looked like oil. Had the surveyor's body been found, or was it pickling in one of these drums?

They walked down a long gravel path towards a shed. Mrs Morrison held the end of her dupatta over her nose and mouth. It was dark inside, and coming from the glare of the courtyard, they waited for their eyes to adjust. They could see a few large pieces of leather stretched and drying on a line. The stench of chemicals drove them out quickly. 'Nothing of interest,' he said, eager to get going, 'it's only a drying shed.' He was convinced that Lal Prasad was planning to murder them, thanks to Mrs Morrison and her incendiary questions. He looked at her with a mixture of irritation and impatience. 'You shouldn't have spoken to Mr Lal Prasad like that.'

'Like what?' she said. 'I merely asked a few straightforward questions.'

No sooner were they back on the gravel path, when they saw two men in green uniforms coming directly towards them. One of them pointed a finger, as though identifying them to his companion. 'You were told to wait at the house,' he shouted in Hindi. 'You cannot wander around. This is not a public garden!' There was no mistaking the menacing, needling tone of the man's voice. 'We must arrest you.'

'Sorry,' Girnar said to the man. 'I'm so sorry. We didn't mean any harm. We came to meet Lal Prasad. But, we're leaving…'

'Who is she?' the man said. 'Does she have a passport? Hand over her passport.'

Girnar whispered to Mrs Morrison, 'We shouldn't have come here. Come on, let's go.' To the man and his companion, Girnar could only nod, too scared to say anything. The men were twenty feet away but gaining on them.

'You're right,' Mrs Morrison said. 'Let's get out of here.' Her voice was tinged with anxiety and Girnar was glad she finally understood the dire situation they were in.

They made their way towards the main gates, and just past the house, broke into a sprint with the two men chasing behind, shouting at them. A few workers, piqued by the commotion, joined in with shouts. Fortunately, the gates were open, a small van was entering and the guard was chatting with the van driver. Girnar and Mrs Morrison dashed in front of the van and cleared the gates.

Once outside, they couldn't find their rickshaw driver. Girnar had asked him to wait, but the man must have found another fare. They kept walking, hoping to see him around the corner, relaxing under a tree. Except for a structure in the distance that looked like a power grid tower there was nothing else around.

Girnar was relieved to be out of the tannery. But now he worried about not finding a rickshaw and missing the train to Haridwar. If a car or a lorry went by, he could flag it down and ask for a lift.

Past the tower the road dipped towards the river and they came upon a small boarded-up building. 'What do you suppose this is?' she said, 'Should we take a look?'

'No!' he said, 'It's just an old building. We must get back to the station…' But she was already down the short path that led to the building.

'It's an old boat house,' she said excitedly.

He stood where he was, watching as she took a few photos. She disappeared behind some trees, and a few moments later, he heard her say, 'You must come and see this!'

He sighed loudly. He might as well take a look at whatever it was she had discovered.

There was no door, only a framed opening, and part of the back wall was missing. Behind the broken wall, the river gleamed, sunlight lazing over the water. A rusty bicycle leaned against a post, and other than a few pieces of machinery and two empty crates turned over on their sides, the place was empty.

'What is it?' he said.

She put a finger to her lips, a gesture for him to be silent.

The building was small and they were standing close together in the centre next to an odd-shaped machine, blackened with oil and covered in years of dirt. It might have been the engine of an upturned boat he could see on the riverbank.

She turned to him slowly, her face open and sincere. 'How peaceful it is here,' she said, her voice heavy with import. 'This is what I love about India, this stillness. I've never felt this anywhere else in the world.'

'Stillness?' he said. Had she forgotten the danger at the tannery they had negotiated not even a half hour ago?

They stared at each other and suddenly she drifted into his arms, her body supple and charged against his. A steady cross draft came in through the doorway and the broken wall at the back. His heart beat fast, in anticipation and fear. What if someone came for the bicycle, what if someone wanted to rig the engine to the boat? She must have sensed his trepidation, for she turned her head and squinted in the direction of the doorway. Her ear against his lips was small and pale, the tiny pearl earring startling in its simplicity against her skin. Waves of anxiety rose from the soles of his feet and spread upward through his body as he held her against his chest. He had no idea what she meant by *the stillness of India*, but he didn't care.

A few moments later they were on the dusty cement floor of the boat house. His heart pulsed loudly and his eyes kept darting around the building. He undid his belt and the top button of his pants, his fingers shaking uncontrollably. 'I've never done this before,' he blurted, and immediately wished he'd kept quiet. She adjusted herself on the floor to a half sitting position, peeled off her salwar and underwear and pulled him closer. She started touching and massaging him in the most urgent, intimate way, and he was shocked and excited and completely beside himself as he fumbled his hands over her breasts and then nudged her legs apart.

He saw the Ganges and heard the lapping water, and when he closed his eyes he smelled the burnt oil of the boat engine and the perspiration of their bodies and the faint citrus scent of Mrs Morrison's soap.

When they finally stood up, she laughed nervously as she dusted herself off, and then modestly turned away to compose herself. He noticed her hands were shaking as she reached behind her back to hook her brassiere, which was beige, and he was enthralled with the knowledge that it had a stitch of lace and a small bow in the front.

As soon as she was dressed, she was all business-like and practical. 'We'd better find a way back to the station,' she said, 'or we'll be stuck here all night.'

Girnar smiled. He pictured the two of them spending the night in the boat house, the ruined building that harboured the stillness of India!

They started walking along the road, hoping to find a rickshaw. Girnar wondered if he should put his arm around her shoulders. After half a kilometre they flagged down a man on a scooter who said he would send an auto-rickshaw for them. Sure enough, within five minutes a rickshaw came sputtering down the road.

Mrs Morrison was quiet in the rickshaw on the way back to the train station. Girnar, sitting beside her on the cracked vinyl seat, was no longer worried about his leg touching hers. He noticed his heart settling into a more normal rhythm. Her foreignness and the fact that she was leaving India the next day should have been monumental concerns, but when he glanced at her, it was enough that a woman like her thought he was somebody. *The stillness of India*—the phrase resounded triumphantly in his head.

She was hungry, so they went back to the same restaurant near the station and this time she ordered the rice-curry plate and he ordered tea and parathas. 'We'd better eat quickly,' he said once the food arrived. 'The train will be leaving soon.'

After they found their seats on the train, he said, 'Can you believe it? We went to a place where someone was murdered, and we actually spoke to the murderer…'

'It's not certain that Lal Prasad is guilty.'

'Have you always been fearless, Mrs Morrison?'

Her face grew contemplative. 'I've lost two toes to frostbite attempting Mount Everest. But I want to try again. I'm not sure if that makes me fearless or stubborn.'

He gazed at her canvas shoes. If he married her, he would have a wife with missing toes.

~

The train stopped briefly at Garhmukteswar, and he wanted to tell Mrs Morrison about this important town: Here, according to legend, the Ganges had taken human form, married King Shantanu, and given birth to eight sons. Seven of them drowned in the river, the eighth, Bhishma, survived and became the hero of the great epic, the *Mahabharata*. But Mrs Morrison was fast asleep, her hands clasped in her lap around her notebook, her head leaning heavily on the window's crossbar.

The train swept into Haridwar station well past midnight. On the platform, human forms stretched out on cane mats against the wall appeared undisturbed by the commotion of the train's arrival. On the way to the hotel, the rickshaw driver gave curt explanations about 'one way' and 'no entry' on a suspiciously roundabout route to deposit them outside a big wrought-iron gate, the entrance to their hotel.

Inside, he argued with the check-in clerk for charging Mrs Morrison double the amount for her room. 'Foreign dollar tax,' the clerk insisted. Girnar had half a mind to say they were 'Mr and Mrs'...but everyone else from his group was in this very hotel. How stupid he had been, he should have suggested they go elsewhere. They could have shared a room, a bed; they could have spent the night naked in each other's arms.

He walked her to her door, with the porter following close behind with her luggage. He wished her 'goodnight' in a formal tone and ambled away to his room.

His suitcase was waiting at the foot of the bed, and after washing and changing, he contemplated going to her room. He could be careful in the hallway.

When he knocked on her door, there was no answer.

He stood there for a while, desire and anxiety propelling his wait. He looked at the room number—yes, it was the correct room. She must be asleep, he decided. After glancing up and down the hallway, he knocked again, a little louder. He put his fingers around the door handle and pressed down slowly, thrilling at the idea of surprising her. Once inside he would strip off his clothes and slip into bed beside her. But the door was locked. He released the handle and, for a brief insane moment, wanted to kick the door down.

He returned to his room, feeling empty and dejected. Sitting on the bed with a pillow propped behind him, he opened a notebook to a clean page. His mind was blank except for this lone thought: tomorrow she was leaving. She was journeying to Delhi, and from there, to London. He had tried coaxing her to stay in the good-natured way one might coax a friend, and when that didn't work he had tried a professional angle. 'Don't you want to see whether the source of the Ganges is pure or polluted?' But Mrs Morrison had another assignment to work on, another country to go to. He put away the notebook. What was the point in writing stories? What was the point in doing anything when the novelty of the past few days was about to end? Everything was slipping away. He had held her in his arms and made love to her, but it seemed so long ago. He turned off the light, got into bed, and lay in the dark thinking about the life he had still somehow to live.

7

Girnar walked beside Mrs Morrison down the long crowded platform to the ladies' compartment. He had met her only five days earlier in Benares, but after what happened at the tannery, he was certain they had been more than friends in a previous lifetime. When he told her this, she drew back a little, looked at him despairingly, and then offered a small smile.

With the stationmaster's whistle, passengers boarded, coolies shouted for no reason, those who couldn't afford a ticket were already shrouded in blankets or sheets, like odd-shaped luggage, on the roof of the train. It was a cool brisk morning, the rays of the sun slowly colouring the sky.

Mrs Morrison settled herself at a window seat in her compartment. 'Please write,' she said to Girnar, standing on the platform. 'You have my address?'

'Yes,' he said, bowing his head slightly.

'Someday, if you come to London…'

An excited tremor rushed through him. He hoped for some assurance from her, a promise of a future happiness. Should he mention his intentions now? He looked around the platform: a bent old coolie limping away, a sweeper woman sitting on her haunches picking at her broom. Not now. He would write a long, eloquent letter and make a formal proposition. He would include a photo of himself, without a bandage, wearing a new suit and tie. The train pitched back a little before lurching forward, and he started walking alongside.

'Mrs Morrison,' he said, and there was no stopping this foolhardy proposal now. 'I would like to marry you.'

'What!'

'Yes,' he said, placing a hand on his chest and quickening his steps to keep up with the train. 'We will be a family, you and me and your daughter, Adela. The three of us! I promise to look after you.'

Mrs Morrison laughed. 'You're joking…'

'No,' he said. 'This was meant to be. Don't you see?' The rushing rhythm of his heart and the clamour in his limbs told him he was on the edge of greatness.

'But…that was one time. I don't know what came over us.' Her face tightened. 'We really shouldn't have…'

'Mrs Morrison,' he was running beside the train now. 'I wanted to marry you before then. I've always wanted to marry you. What do you say? It is in your hands. We can live in London or New York or anywhere you want. We can live here in Haridwar, in a house on the banks of the Ganges.'

Shaking her head, she looked away briefly. And then, 'Of course!' she yelled, a brilliant smile filling her face, 'Why not? We should get married!'

He nodded happily, running faster to keep up. 'We will climb Everest together!' he shouted.

She leaned to the window with an urgent expression, but it was impossible to make out her words.

He kept running alongside the train, grinning and

waving, until the end of the platform, and then he stood on the grade that went down to the tracks with his hands on his hips, breathing heavily, until the last of the train cars disappeared against the slowly brightening sky.

~

The Ganges descended from the Siwalik Hills, the last gentle slopes of the Himalayas, into the plains at Haridwar with quiet, calculated stealth. Countless years ago, Vishnu, Preserver of the Universe, had carelessly left his footprint in a mammoth rock near the water's edge. Shops at the top of the ghats sold imitations of the footprint impressed in black stone.

Standing at Brahm Kund ghat, Girnar was amazed at how narrow the river was here. He could throw a rock to the other side. But the current…he touched his bandaged head and stared in fascination as the river sped forth, heedless of anything in her path.

As dusk inched over Haridwar, crowds pressed close to the water on either bank, preparing to float thousands of oil lamps for the evening prayer. Girnar elbowed his way past hawkers selling colourful powders, saffron-robed saints with prayer beads, and men in blue uniforms with receipt books collecting donations. He bought an oil lamp from a small shop. It came in a bowl-shaped packet wrapped in leaves stitched together with white thread. Inside there was a wick surrounded by flowers, a tiny matchbox, and an incense stick.

He made his way back to the riverbank just as loudspeakers announced the start of prayers. There was a brief, deep silence before everyone started chanting, celebrating the river goddess and asking for her blessings.

He held a match to the wick, and with the flickering light falling on his face, joined in the chanting.

When the prayers ended he bent towards the water, cradling the lamp in both palms. The Ganges was a headstrong goddess, but she paused now, as though to acknowledge his offering. He stood up slowly, his eyes intent on the flame as it floated away in the current, a dot mingling with a thousand and one others. The river dazzled and danced, but he knew she had no time to stay and sit and feast. Too soon the lamps dimmed and the river grew dark. Girnar gazed into the darkness, breathing evenly, and felt in his veins the quiet sensation of the passage of time.

~

Leaving the riverbank, he hailed an auto-rickshaw. He couldn't wait to get back to the hotel and to his room, to think quietly about Mrs Morrison. The night was cool and dry and he felt comforted by the slow rumble of traffic and the glare of headlamps around him. The sudden appearance of the moon, a huge silver arc almost touching the rooftops, affirmed to him that his life had taken on a new cadence. He sat back in the rickshaw, in the middle of the seat with arms outstretched and began singing snippets of Hindi songs.

'Are you drunk?' the rickshawallah asked, glancing over his shoulder.

'No,' he said indignantly, and then lapsed into silence.

While they stopped at a traffic signal, the rickshawallah waved to someone inside a brightly lit teashop at the opposite corner. 'The chaiwallah is my friend,' he said to Girnar. 'It's a good teashop. Even big politicians come here.'

Girnar squinted at the teashop and imagined Niranjan

sitting at one of the outdoor tables. Niranjan had some aspirations of running for Parliament, but Girnar couldn't picture him as a politician. According to Girnar's father, most of the politicians in India were corrupt: 'A gang of crooks and frauds. Only thinking about the next election… getting carried away by the sound of their own voices and the hollow applause of groundlings.' But Niranjan didn't strike Girnar as the dishonest type. A plastic canopy covered the area outside the teashop and pieces of gunnysack hung on one side, partitioning the shop from the eatery next door. A stray dog nosed through a heap of rubbish between the two establishments. Niranjan was a stylish man; he would take tea at a fancier place, Girnar concluded.

The rickshaw sped down a tree-lined road, bouncing over potholes, the noisy motor rasping and shuddering.

Girnar tapped the rickshawallah's shoulder. 'Stop at a place that sells liquor.'

'No place in Haridwar sells liquor.'

Girnar slumped back into the seat. In Ahmedabad, some of his colleagues frequented a restaurant called Kingfisher that sold a homemade concoction that resembled beer. They'd invited him once, but he had declined. Upon returning to Ahmedabad, he decided to treat his colleagues to drinks and announce his forthcoming marriage. He couldn't wait to see their envious faces as he told them about Mrs Morrison.

Suddenly the rickshawallah did a nimble U-turn. 'There is one place,' he said, grinning at him over his shoulder. He dropped Girnar outside a shabby apartment building. 'Go to the second floor,' he said, 'the staircase is at the back. I will wait for you here.'

There were mostly college boys and girls up there, playing cards and drinking, and they looked at him curiously. The owner, a hefty man in a turban, led him to a filthy kitchen, and set a glass for him on the counter. He called it whisky, but it was pink and tasted sweet. He introduced Girnar to his wife, a tall woman in a glittery sari, who was frying something at the stove.

Girnar sat with his drink on a sagging sofa in a narrow passageway that led from the kitchen to the dining room. He could hear the college kids joking and betting on their cards and every now and again he saw the tall woman at the end of the passageway, like a shiny apparition floating in the cigarette smoke.

When the turbaned man asked if he wanted another drink, he said, 'Why not?' After a while his glittery wife came with a plate of fried chillies and sat on the sofa with Girnar. Dipped in thick yellow batter, the chillies left a taste of stale oil in his mouth. After taking the empty plate from his hand, and setting it on the floor, she moved closer. In a swift easy gesture she put her leg over his knee and let her sari fall off her shoulder. Part of the sari lay bunched in his lap and he stared down at it, mesmerized by the tiny sparkling sequins. She touched a finger to his chin, while her other hand kept moving over his thigh. The bedroom was air-conditioned, she said, and she could open a bottle of imported whisky.

'Oh,' he said, and stood up hurriedly. In the kitchen he left some money on the counter, edged his way to the door, and then stumbled down the stairs, holding the railing with both hands.

He found the rickshaw driver and returned to the hotel

somewhat dazed. The rest of the night could have easily been spent in reveries of his new life with Mrs Morrison but he felt compelled to work on his stories. He threw open the windows, the sky was a blanket of stars, and as he wrote he listened to the night, to the owls and tree frogs, and to the river that was always breathing with him.

8

Pink whisky and fried chillies did not agree with Girnar. His head ached and his stomach was writhing as he boarded the mini bus. While writing, his heaving stomach had sent him to the bathroom, and it was there, with his bowels exploding in the toilet and vomit rising in his throat, that he had spent most of the night.

He sat alone at the back of the bus, closed his eyes, but couldn't sleep. It started raining, an energetic downpour. Krishnan, the bus driver, could barely see, only one wiper was working and it moved sluggishly. At places the road flooded and the bus could only crawl forward.

They drove past a pharmaceutical factory, chemical and fertilizer complexes, and an oil refinery. Where were these factories dumping their waste? Mrs Morrison would be in Delhi by now. In a few hours she would go to the airport. Recalling the playful look on her face as the train left the station in Haridwar, and her parting words—*Of course, we should get married*—he smiled through his headache. As clouds of heroism hovered over him, he felt empowered in his mission to clean up the Ganges. He would create a new environmental ethos in India.

The thought struck him like a thunderbolt. Mrs Morrison had no intentions of marrying him. He remembered what he had told her—*In India we say 'yes' to everything, it promotes hope.* The sudden realization was like a kick in the gut, and he felt the blood coursing through his veins. There was no denying it, she had agreed too quickly. He felt demoralized and stupid at his impetuousness. There was no chance of them getting married, she'd agreed to his proposal only to repel his disappointment. He remained morose and silent for a long time, comforted mildly by the settling of his queasy stomach.

~

As they approached Rishikesh, the rain abated. A pantheon of images—Rama, Sita, Ganesh, Hanuman, Saraswati—were painted on walls of ashrams, and pasted on posters around the city. At a traffic signal he stared into a shop selling conch shells, miniature idols, and lithographs, and imagined Mrs Morrison inside the shop.

There was no desk in his room at the Ganges View Hotel, but he was happy to have a small balcony overlooking the river just fifty metres away. The water, broad and swift, was full of big mahseer fish—golden-green with large heads and thin bodies. He watched a group of young boys throwing handfuls of puffed rice into the water. The white kernels hovered in the wind before the fish jumped to the surface. Leaving the balcony door open, he stretched out on the bed. Again, his thoughts turned to Mrs Morrison. He could hear the river rumbling along and he pictured the fish gliding with the current.

When he awoke a few hours later, Jadu was sitting outside his door. He handed him a note from Niranjan: he was to meet the group at Chotiwalla's restaurant.

Cows and stray dogs roved the bazaar. People wandered

in and out of shops. He was wearing blue cotton pants and a white shirt with sleeves rolled up. He walked slowly along the footpath, his hands in his pocket. A man sitting on a low stool on the side of the road whistled and waved at him. He was selling medicinal roots, touted to cure diseases from dyspepsia and diabetes to heart ailments. 'For your head,' he said, choosing a brown fibrous clump and pointing it to his bandage. 'Mash with Ganges water and apply twice daily.' Girnar shook his head and kept walking. 'Bilva root is favoured by Shiva,' the man called after him.

He came upon Laxman Jhoola, the footbridge named after a hero of the *Ramayana*. Built of braided metal cables strung taut and anchored into huge stone pylons on either side of the shore, it was supposedly the exact spot where Laxman crossed the river many centuries ago. The bridge swayed with the constant stream of people. It was a grand engineering feat, and Girnar wanted to feel inspired by it; instead, he looked upon the whole thing with dulled interest. He ventured across, jostling his way through the crowd, stood on the other bank for a few minutes, and then jostled his way back.

Not wanting to see the medicine man again, he wandered along the river past a row of ashrams. Outside a large yellow building, he took in the transcendental scents of rose and sandalwood incense, and couldn't help but smile at the signboard: *One Month Enlightenment Course*, and below, *Easy Sanskrit Without Grammar.*

The bathing ghats here were crumbling cement steps disappearing into the swollen river. A foreign man in swimming shorts was in the water, clutching the rusted metal railing as the water swirled around his ankles. Girnar looked at him and wanted to ask whether he was enrolled in 'Easy Sanskrit,' but he only nodded and walked on.

He managed to find Chotiwalla's restaurant. A pot-bellied man, his body painted pink, in a blue dhoti and heavy gilt jewellery, sat at the entrance. The choti, a sprout of hair oiled to a four-inch point, rose rocket-like from his head. He looked for Niranjan and the others, but couldn't see them. Perhaps they had already eaten and left. Girnar found a table at the back and forgetting his earlier resolve for a simple meal, studied the menu carefully and ordered a feast.

When he returned to the hotel, he ran into Samira on the verandah overlooking the back garden. He had the awkward feeling he was interrupting her; he stepped forward and let the door close behind him.

'Professor-ji, we didn't see you all day,' Samira said. 'Are you all right?'

Moths spiralled around the dim light bulbs on the verandah. The night was cool and breezy. Now and then, over the roar of the river, came the drone of drums and the blast of truck horns from the highway a few kilometres away.

'I'm all right,' he said, slouching into a chair near her with a heavy sigh. He looked towards the rushing Ganges. Writing stories was tiring work, and now he didn't see the point of it anymore. He wanted to take all the notebooks—there were more than a dozen of them now—and dump them in the river. For nothing he had wasted his time all these nights. Even Samira had stopped asking about his stories. She was in a red sari, and her hair looked nice, all wavy and puffed in a clip.

He stared openly at Samira. How stupid he had been to ignore her all these years. In Ahmedabad, he saw her almost every day, outside the lift, sometimes at the corner market or the bus stop. If only he had paid attention to her.

'By the way, Professor-ji,' she said casually, 'are you still writing stories? You must have written dozens of pages by now.' At the beginning of the pilgrimage she was sceptical of his project, but now he detected confidence and expectation in her voice.

His heart raced. 'My stories?' he said. 'Of course. I'm writing them for you...' He stopped himself, and turned away in embarrassment. He stood up and fumbled in his pocket for his key. 'Goodnight. I must finish writing.'

9

Travelling north from Rishikesh, a little beyond Uttarkashi, the Ganges disappeared. Girnar recalled Mrs Morrison telling him about the great Tehri Dam. Constructed from rock-fill and earth, it created a reservoir with a surface area of fifty-two square kilometres. Although the dam provided power and water for irrigation and drinking all the way to Delhi, its construction had submerged dozens of villages and destroyed vast areas of forests and farmlands. For several moments he imagined Mrs Morrison; the milky pallor of her skin and the dash of colour which leapt to her cheeks when she spoke about the river.

As the road spiralled up the mountain, Girnar caught a glimpse of the vast expanse of water falling and foaming in thick white sheets. He would have liked to stand at the base of the dam and hear the thunderous roar. Alongside the dam, several trucks raised clouds of dust as they crawled over the denuded land and construction workers moved like ants over zigzag ramps. He guessed it was some sort of dam expansion project.

The bus lumbered steadily upward, and here and there in the soft rock he could see the bite marks of bulldozers that had built the road. Pines, deodars and flowering shrubs scattered the mountainside. Billboards warned: *Drive Rash,*

End in Crash, This is Highway, Not Runway; one with a cartoonish image of a car skidding into a deep ravine said, *Going Faster Leads to Disaster.*

At places the bus crunched over long patches of gravel, sending plumes of dust in its wake. From a path above the road, two boys prodding a herd of mules strapped with firewood, waved at the bus. Girnar waved back, but realized they couldn't see him through the tinted windows.

They stopped for lunch at a tourist lodge, a large stone building with the Indian flag fluttering on top. He could see the Ganges, a blue-green swirl, in the gorges below. The lodge was crowded and the menu on the chalkboard listed four items: Small Breakfast, Big Breakfast, Lunch, and Dinner.

After lunch as they headed back to the bus, he approached Samira. 'Come and sit at the back,' he said, in the most casual tone he could muster.

'I feel nauseated at the back of the bus,' she said.

Girnar climbed aboard, shuffled along the aisle and slumped down in the last row, spreading out in both seats. He leaned his body closer to the window. His eyes fell on two foreign tourists outside, a middle-aged couple just arriving at the lodge in a car. The man got out and stretched while the woman stood talking to the driver. Mrs Morrison must have reached London by now. He wondered if she lived in a house or a flat. From photos and movies, London seemed a staid, spare version of Ahmedabad, at odds with the exciting, spirited woman to whom he had foolishly proposed. Both of them on the floor of the boat house—he wondered if she thought of that as often as he did—or, did she chalk it up as part of the adventure of India? No, not 'adventure.' What had she called it? He smiled as he recalled her words: *the stillness of India.*

Samira was nudging his shoulder. 'Professor-ji, can you move, please?'

He shot to his feet and his heart raced as he slid toward the window. As the bus swung onto the main road, he watched Samira pull a black cardigan over her cream-coloured salwar kameez. 'It'll get cold soon,' she said. 'Have you brought woollens?' He stared at her hands, mesmerized by the way she buttoned the cardigan and then flipped the cuffs over her wrists. He glanced at the small pearl buttons at her chest.

She was enjoying the pilgrimage, she said, and not looking forward to returning home. Within a month she had to sit for a board exam. But Girnar could tell from the way she described her research project on DNA sequencing and monoclonal antibodies that she was passionate about her profession. The terms she used were all foreign to him, but he listened with interest. 'Don't you get tired,' he asked, 'of looking into a microscope all day? You should have become a real doctor.' She looked at him severely. 'I *am* a real doctor,' she said, and went on to explain analyzing blood and human tissue was no small matter. Girnar smiled at her temerity and confidence.

'What about your stories?' she said.

As the bus roared uphill, he recounted the plots, described the characters and their motives.

Samira held her breath at key points in the narration and his heart soared at the encouragement. Whenever she shook her head or pressed her lips doubtfully, his heart sank. She interrupted him a few times—that couldn't have happened, you've misunderstood the point. 'It's a *story*,' he reiterated each time. 'Okay, okay,' she conceded, and he noticed the dash of admiration that filled her eyes, which were big and clear and coloured with kajal.

She wanted to read his stories and although his heart skipped in panic, he agreed. 'But not now…' he added. He must make sure there was no mention in his stories of Mrs Morrison.

'Whenever you're ready,' she said, laughing lightly.

As the road got steeper, the bus slowed and shuddered to a lower gear. 'Are you all right?' he asked, noticing her pale, stricken face.

She shook her head and leaned back in the seat.

'Close your eyes,' he suggested. 'Sleep for a while. We should be there soon.'

As the bus turned a corner, her head fell on his shoulder. A delightful shock rushed over him and he stared straight in front.

They had just passed Harsil, the last hamlet before Gangotri, when Krishnan pulled over. He felt lightheaded, the driver said, and directed Arjunesh to take the wheel. Arjunesh was hesitant; he'd only recently got his driving licence. While Krishnan and Arjunesh argued, Girnar glanced at Samira's head on his shoulder and hoped she wouldn't wake up. Her dark silky hair smelled of herbal shampoo.

Arjunesh, who was wearing a loud yellow shirt, took the driver's seat. He produced a pair of sunglasses from his pocket. Putting them on, he looked back at the passengers and grinned. The moment he turned the key in the ignition, a pain bolted through Girnar's head, starting at the centre and travelling in a short quick zap to the wound on his forehead. A few days ago, before going to the exhibition grounds with Mrs Morrison, he had experienced this exact sensation.

Arjunesh drove the bus as though it was a sports car. He overtook cars and trucks on hairpin bends with no guardrails. Girnar raised an arm and held on to the sleeping Samira. The brakes squealed—and then it happened. The bus began sliding sideways, the rear spinning out to the right. The front hit some large boulders at the edge of the road, throwing the bus to the left and slamming it against the mountain. Samira was jolted awake. Shock and fear covered her face as he held on to her with both arms. The windows rattled and the screams inside the bus grew louder as metal scraped against rock. An oncoming truck honked furiously and tried to swerve out of the way, but it hit the same boulders at an angle. Girnar watched in horror as the truck rose in the air and flew headlong over the embankment. A huge plume of dust, a few seconds of intense silence, and then a loud sound of crushing metal faded away like an echo.

Their bus skidded off the road, bounced to the edge, and came to rest sideways in a shallow ditch against the mountain. There was a stunned hush inside the bus for a moment, and then everyone was shouting and screaming. A fiery smell of rubber and tar filled the air.

By the time they all climbed out, two other cars and another tourist bus had pulled over. Gathered at the edge, everyone looked for the truck, which had plunged hundreds of feet into the ravine.

There might have been a slick of oil or even a patch of

ice on the road, and Arjunesh might have tried to steer in the direction of the skid; nobody knew for sure. But they knew he was an inexperienced driver who was driving too fast. Arjunesh was throwing his hands in the air and weeping loudly. Krishnan was examining the bus, which was damaged on one side, the front tyre hissing and almost flat, headlamps shattered, and the metal so badly dented it was impossible to make out the swirl of silver painted over the blue on the side of the bus. There was not a scratch on any of the passengers.

Several policemen, dressed in army uniforms, arrived in two Jeeps. They barricaded the road with stones and orange flags. Two policemen attempted to climb to the truck but a few metres down they were slipping and sliding, sending a shower of rocks and dirt into the ravine. Their supervisor called them off. The rescue, if the driver had survived, would have to wait until proper equipment was brought up from Uttarkashi or Rishikesh.

The supervisor told everyone to go, there was nothing more to be done at the side of the road, Gangotri was about a kilometre that way, and they could walk there easily. Everyone stood around for a few more minutes—all of them feeling useless and terrified and undeservedly fortunate. Niranjan took charge, waving and herding everyone up the road, and they walked to town in silence.

~

Gangotri, at an elevation of 11,000 feet, was where King Bhagiratha had performed his penances to urge the Ganges down from the heavens. The river was called Bhagirathi here. There was a temple, built of white granite blocks and silver domes, at the spot where the king had sat in meditation.

Snow-capped Himalayan peaks loomed around Gangotri. Resthouses and small shrines lined the way from the bus station to the big temple. Four or five tea stalls with wooden benches were packed with customers. A man holding a clipboard marched around selling tickets for a guided trek to the Gaurikund Falls. Pilgrims in shawls and sweaters milled about in the small bazaar where shops sold odds and ends. Film music blared from one of the shops.

Standing outside the temple in a snaking queue with the rest of the group, Girnar felt a flutter of dizziness. It was the altitude; in a few hours his body would adjust. A man approached them for donations to help feed the monkeys—their food supply, he explained, was severely compromised because of the felled trees, and in the past few years more and more monkeys were getting sick and dying. Girnar was struck by the man's earnestness and by his sad, lonely demeanour. He handed him some money and the man smiled as he handed him a leaflet about monkeys along with a receipt.

Samira asked if he was going to write about the road accident. He shrugged and looked at her, puzzled. Did she remember falling asleep on the bus, her head touching his shoulder? Did she remember how fast and urgently he had held her in his arms as the bus slammed the side of the mountain? Did she realize there was a serious bond between them now?

The Gangotri temple housed a deity of Goddess Ganga, a serene beauty sitting cross-legged and erect on a crocodile, one hand raised heavenward, the other outstretched with fingers curled downward, bestowing her blessings upon the world. As the temple bells chimed in sequence, and the peal of gongs and conch shells rent the air, Girnar bowed his head reverentially, but he couldn't stop thinking of Samira.

~

Niranjan led the way to their hotel, a tourist bungalow a short walk from town. All the rooms opened onto a long common verandah arranged with old wicker sofas and tables. Although Niranjan had booked the whole bungalow, with the road blocked there weren't enough rooms for the group—a few people from an earlier party had had to stay on until they could resume their journey. Girnar had to share a room with Niranjan. Their room had two cots pushed against the walls with barely a foot of space between.

There was time before dinner, so Girnar decided to go for a walk. He knocked on Samira's door, but there was no answer. He set off alone, taking the road back into town, following a cracked, cement path downhill. Nothing except a few scraggly shrubs covered the ground and he could see the river a few metres away, a wide stunning crystalline torrent.

He followed the river downstream, picking his way over white and grey boulders scattered along the bank. The atmosphere was lyrical and symphonic as though the river was singing a joyous song. Around a bend, the water cascaded dramatically into large pools. At places it had sprayed onto the overhanging rocks and frozen into dagger-like ice formations.

He looked up the path in the direction of the town and saw cement walls, billboards, metal roofs, and strings of triangular prayer flags. The Himalayan glaciers had taken more than ten thousand years to form. What would happen to the Ganges a few centuries from now? The Saraswati, the lost river of India, existed now only in people's belief and in ancient Hindu texts.

A middle-aged man in a red overcoat was filling a plastic bottle with water. He waved at Girnar. 'Have you tried the water?' he shouted.

Girnar shook his head and waved back. 'Is it cold?'

'Minus four Celsius,' the man said with a laugh, and then took a swig from the bottle. 'Did you hear about the bus accident?' he asked.

Girnar continued walking. As they neared the town, the man caught up with him. 'A blue mini-bus,' he said. 'It skidded off the road and went over the ravine.' He mimed the skid with his hand. 'The army people pulled it out with a crane. It was finished. Everyone inside died.'

Bewildered at the story, Girnar told him what had really happened.

'It was the truck driver's time to go,' the man said. 'But you got some injury?' He pointed to Girnar's bandaged head.

When Girnar explained his injury was not from the bus accident, the man looked disappointed. He informed Girnar that the water had medicinal properties.

'Yes, I know,' Girnar said.

'You should drink it every day,' he said, pointing again to Girnar's bandaged head.

Girnar quickened his pace. He was tired of everyone commenting on his injury.

'See,' the man continued, 'My blood pressure was high for many years, but for two weeks I've been drinking Ganges water, and guess what? This morning my pressure was one-twenty over seventy. Good, no? Also, the water is full of minerals that aid digestion. I have no more constipation. Every morning…'

'That's very good,' Girnar said, and hurried off.

~

After Niranjan was asleep, Girnar slipped out of the room, notebooks tucked under his arm. He was worried about reviewing his stories, a little afraid of what he might discover in them. If they didn't pass muster, how could he show them to Samira? He couldn't afford their relationship to unravel on account of his mediocre imagination.

On the verandah, he positioned a chair directly below the fluorescent light. The cushions sagged and the wicker creaked as he pulled his legs up. He had a sweater over his pajamas and a woollen cap over his bandage. He wished he had worn socks.

Beyond the verandah the night was dark and still, and as he started reading, there was no sound except for the distant roar of the river hurtling down the mountain.

10

Only five of them continued on to Gaumukh. Halfway along the eighteen-kilometre trek to the glacier, the air was already too thin for most of the party. It would only get worse at 14,000 feet. They had hired five coolies and now two of them would climb with the small group to Gaumukh. They would camp for the night at Bhojbasa, before the final ascent to the glacier. 'Here,' Girnar said to Samira, who had decided against joining the final ascent. Handing her his notebooks, he said, 'Here are my stories.'

'I'll wait for you at Gangotri,' she said, taking the notebooks. 'You'll be careful?'

He took her hand and pressed it lightly to his chest. They stood quietly, both of them unsure of what to say. Samira was more fetching than ever. A pathologist, no less…they could discuss the biology of the Ganges and waterborne diseases…there would be plenty of time later. All he had to do right now was make it to the glacier and back. He was going to the source of the Ganges, for both of them.

As he set off, his heart raced. He felt like a film hero when he turned to wave and saw Samira wave back, her face full of worry for him. The trail climbed steadily uphill before levelling off to a long, rock-covered plain with patches of muddy snow. He trudged along quietly, wondering if he should have stayed back with Samira. He counted the hours until he would see her again. When the pilgrimage was over he would write to Mrs Morrison. She would be pleased to hear he had decided on an Indian bride.

Feeling lighthearted, he chatted with his four companions, pointing out the beauty of this or that peak or waterfall along the way. Donkeys traipsed past with firewood in panniers slung over their backs. They saw a pair of Himalayan serow goats scampering around the rocks. Niranjan said there were snow leopards in the area, and he kept on the lookout for them.

When they arrived at Bhojbasa, an elevation of 13,000 feet, the coolies led them past the town, which comprised a few huts, a meteorological office, and a temple, to a large ledge jutting from the mountainside. At first Girnar wondered why the coolies had brought them to this desolate spot, but when he looked out, he understood why: in the distance, directly across their campsite, the Bhagirathi peak, 22,000 feet high, stood noble and spectacular, the shadowy north face of the mountain tinged pink in the waning afternoon light. Below them, a thin fog was rolling into the valley.

That evening he visited a temple near the campsite. It was a rustic structure with no walls, only six pillars supporting a metal roof. Kerosene lamps lit up the perimeter and about a dozen people sat cross-legged on the floor. There was a deity at the altar, but it was impossible to make out its face. Girnar was moved by the simplicity of the place. The people started singing, their faces silhouetted against the dark cold evening. The sincerity of their voices reminded him of an old Vedic myth claiming the gods and goddesses were born from verses and music.

11

They awoke early to start for Gaumukh. There was a long day ahead, because after Gaumukh they would have to trek downhill all the way to Gangotri before nightfall. They had eaten a simple breakfast of tea and porridge cooked over an open fire when an old man appeared at the campsite. He wore a faded orange dhoti and despite the frigid weather his upper body was bare. The holy yellow tilak was freshly painted on his forehead. He had given up everything, he said. He had no family, no connections, nothing of worldly value to recommend him. He told the group he trekked to Gaumukh routinely. The river was cold there, he admitted, but he always jumped in for a few seconds. 'It fortifies the soul,' he said, shutting his eyes and smiling slowly.

Niranjan tried to give him a few rupees to send him away; they had encountered sadhus like these every day of the pilgrimage. But this sadhu bowed his head and refused the money. 'Is it not enough?' Niranjan said, irritated.

The sadhu shook his head; he didn't need money, he had come to give them his blessings.

They bowed perfunctorily as they filed past him.

Girnar admired the sadhu's resilience, and he turned to look at him again. The sadhu held his gaze and called out:

'Those who bathe in the Ganges at Gaumukh will have eternal wisdom.'

~

Other than a scattering of birch trees there was no vegetation on the path up from Bhojbasa. The sun grew bright overhead, the air cold and still. Girnar tried not to think about the bouts of dizziness that came and went. They were swaddled in woollens, but the two coolies wore only thin waistcoats over their clothes, one of them had an old chequered scarf over his ears. Girnar's lips felt chapped and his hands were almost numb despite the new gloves he had bought in Gangotri.

He was panting heavily but keeping a good pace, right behind the coolies. He adjusted the rucksack on his shoulders and continued climbing across the moraine. Banks of rockslides had formed a lateral ridge at one place and it was slow going around the crest. A slight loss of balance, a minor slip of the foot and one could fall thousands of feet into the valley.

Raising a hand to shield his eyes from the sun, Girnar looked up at the high peaks that rose like spires of snow. Here and there streams had gouged through the rocks and channelled crooked ravines. There was something stately and controlled and immortal about the landscape, as though something of immense power had created this tableau.

After a couple of kilometres the path stopped at the edge of a chasm, the ground on either side steep and sludgy. They gathered at the site, staring in awe and disbelief at the abyss below. Niranjan pointed to a place, some distance away, where a weathered plank lay balanced across the chasm. The coolies protested vehemently, invoking the memory of two pilgrims who only a week earlier had tumbled to their deaths in another gorge, right before their eyes. But Niranjan insisted, promising extra baksheesh to the coolies. Niranjan suddenly looked at Girnar, 'What do you think, Professor?'

They'd come too far to turn back and he was eager to fulfil the tacit pledge of heroism he had made with Samira. He glanced at the coolies who were now sitting on their haunches awaiting a decision. Shutting his eyes for a few seconds, he waited to see if the severe pain he had experienced in his head before the riots at the exhibition grounds and the bus accident might come to him now.

'We should go on,' he said.

~

The glacier came into view quite suddenly. Grey and white and brown, it was the colour of the sea and the sky and the earth. The face of the glacier was tilted forward, and under it, from its arch-shaped mouth, poured the Ganges, a pulsing, stunning energy. The scale and grandeur of the sight was nothing like Girnar had imagined. He drew a sharp breath and felt in the marrow of his being the sanctity of beginnings.

Stepping towards a shallow pool, a few metres from the river, he bent over and dipped his fingertips. The water felt like a thousand needles piercing his skin, and he withdrew his hand instantly. *Those who bathe in the river at Gaumukh will have eternal wisdom*, the sadhu had said. Girnar shuddered at the thought. Eternal wisdom was one thing, but what about hypothermia? He scooped water in his canteen and drank a big gulp. A cold ache hit his teeth as the back of his throat went numb.

Standing there, staring at the surging waters, he tried to commit the scene to memory, to describe later to Samira. He looked at his companions who were filling their water bottles or cupping their hands and sipping tentatively. Niranjan was kneeling beside a pool, performing a rudimentary ablution, splashing water on his forehead, cringing each time the water touched his skin. A small chunk of the glacier crashed into the river near the party and everyone except Girnar immediately backed away. 'Professor-ji, it's dangerous. Step back,' Niranjan said, but Girnar was undeterred.

He set aside his rucksack and canteen and clambered up the rocks, trying to get as close to the glacier as he could. Coming upon a flat boulder he stopped to catch his breath. There was nowhere further to go. There, in the cadence of the river, he heard the song and story of the world. It was a sound that would remain in his spirit forever. He was a speck in the cosmos, created not solely by time or history or science or art, but by all these things and also something more. It came to him then, this awareness: he could let go of his ambitions and expectations and draw hope from the process of life itself. The measure of greatness, the essence of wisdom, lay silently at the centre of it all, in the verve and purity of effort. Why had he not known this before? His stories were attempts to describe the lives of others, but it was time to transcend his vain, paltry imaginings and listen to the snow peaks, the rocks, the air and the river. They were the heart of the matter, a story already written by the grandest storyteller. When he returned to his writing, he would remember this stillness; indeed, in the months and years ahead it would empower his work.

There was a quiet pool near the boulder, about four feet

deep, the current diminished by an arc of rocks polished smooth by the water. Behind him Niranjan was shouting, but he could barely hear him over the booming river. Girnar shuffled out of his shoes, peeled off his socks. In a few quick movements, he stripped off his clothes, everything, including his white briefs and the thin bandage on his head, the cold air stinging the wound on his forehead. He stood for a moment, shivering in his nakedness and then, just like that, plunged into the Ganges.

Acknowledgements

This book would not exist were it not for the enthusiasm and expertise of several people. My thanks to Renuka Chatterjee, most deft and insightful editor, as well as Anurag Basnet, Ravi Singh and the fine team at Speaking Tiger.

For the gift of time and place, for knowing that something rich emerges in the collaboration of solitude and uncertainty, I owe a debt of gratitude to Hedgebrook Writer's Retreat and Hawthronden Castle Fellowship.

I'm grateful to the esteemed writers whom I met during my residencies: Ruth Ozeki, Antonya Nelson, Ellen Sussman, Donna Miscolta, Judith Bryan, Helena Drysdale, Rebecca Stot, Tiffany Atkinson, and Kseniya Melnik.

I'm indebted to my circle of literary friends—Kaleta Doolin, Nancy Allen, Jane Saginaw, Donna Wilhelm, and Trea Yip. And, Rita Juster, whose friendship is my true fortune.

My gratitude to the Dallas Institute of Humanities and Culture. Members of the Book Group, thank you for sharing your love of stories. Fellows of the Institute and Members of the Board, I am deeply fortunate to know each of you. Larry Allums, sincere thanks for your confidence and wisdom that continually sustain me.

Thanks to my family and friends who believed in my

passion for fiction and stayed on the journey with me: Harish and Rashmi Chinai, Suryakantam Sanga, Niti and Saurin Patel, Renée Dyer, Jackie Bailey, Jutta and Arie Vanselm, Smita Rao, Angelica Tratter, Freya Bergren, Saadia Khalil, Rosalind de Rolon, Aléjandrina Drew, Esther Ritz, Sudeshna Baksi-Lahiri, Akshat and Lynnda Chinai, Satchit Srinivasan, and Alan Govenar.

I'm grateful to Jai, Kirun, Monica, Sarath, Lindsey and Luciana for being in my life and making it dazzle.

Finally, my thanks to Raghu, who helps bring focus and clarity to every day.

ALSO FROM SPEAKING TIGER

THE EDGE OF ANOTHER WORLD

Pepita Seth

The Edge of Another World is the story of three women living in different times and spaces, whose lives enmesh and interconnect in strange and unforeseen ways.

Shaken by her mother's death, Sophie, a contemporary English woman, accepts the offer of a holiday in Portugal's Alentejo region, at a hotel that was once a convent. Satishan Nambiar, a historian from Malabar in Kerala, tells her about the frescoes in the convent's church and the great megalithic standing stones where Sophie finds the small figure of a Madonna-like Indian goddess. Before they part, Satishan invites her to Malabar...

Born to an unknown mother during the throes of an earthquake in sixteenth-century Portugal, Inês yearns to know her origins. Although taken into a noble family's household, her life changes when Leonor, the family's younger daughter, enters a convent, taking Inês as her servant. When Lucas van Domburg, the painter commissioned to create the frescoes in the church, sees Inês, he declares her to be 'his' Virgin, and insists on using her likeness in the murals. A tragic turn of events leaves Ines alone in Malabar but it is here that she finally discovers her true identity.

In Malabar, Thattakkutty, a Namboodiri Brahmin girl, lives an enclosed and orthodox life in an illam 'a long time ago'. Irked by her intelligence, her guru schemes to destroy her. Simultaneously, rumours begin that her elder sister, Arya-edathi, has an illicit relationship with a Nambiar man. The distraught Arya-edathi dies by her own hand, and as Thattakutty runs to her, she sees that the great doors of the illam are open. She flees out, supported by her Goddess—uniting with her, rushing to meet her own fate.

Years and centuries later, the final drama of Thattakutty's life will affect both Sophie and Ines.

ALSO FROM SPEAKING TIGER

UNCERTAIN LIGHT

Marion Molteno

High in the mountains of war-torn Tajikistan, rebels abduct inspirational UN peace negotiator, Rahul Khan. The lives of his closest friends begin to unravel.

Tessa, now married with two children, has never stopped loving Rahul. Lance, a dedicated aid worker, has used Rahul's friendship to avoid facing up to the gaps in his own life. Hugo, his UN supervisor, feels responsible for the abduction and is driven to uncover the truth. Tajik translator Nargis owes Rahul a personal debt but has secrets she cannot share. As hopes for Rahul's survival fade, each must find a way to begin again.

Set in Central Asia following the collapse of the Soviet Union, *Uncertain Light* vividly evokes a sense of place and an almost tangible atmosphere. With an authenticity and attention to detail that perfectly capture the nuanced compromises of relationships, Marion Molteno deftly weaves the strands of these interlocking worlds into a story of intimacy, hard choices, heartache and courage.

CPSIA information can be obtained
at www.ICGtesting.com
Printed in the USA
LVOW10s0242120917
548294LV00015B/2170/P